Finding

Book Two

Some Love Never Dies

by

J L Appleton

Copyright © Jasmine Appleton 2018

www.jasmine-appleton.co.uk

And at Amazon Books

Coffee Shop
E-mails
The Photograph
Love
Gas
Change of Events
Remembering
Phil
Help
A Friend to Stay
Consequence of Men
Time Goes By
Phil or Danny
The Truth Will Out
A Strange Lunch Date
Dinner Date
Christmas
A Dream

Chapter One
Coffee Shop

Jumping out of bed, Alison was in a rush to start the first day of the rest of her love life, or so she hoped.

Last week she had put the wheels in motion, now she wondered what she had done. She was aware of her breathing, it was fast and she had to stop to take a deep breath and calm herself. She had filled in that online form. The girls seemed to think it was a wonderful idea but now she was losing her nerve.

She opened her coffee shop early that morning as she wanted to get in front of herself with her work load. She had arranged a get together with two of her friends for mid morning coffee and cakes. They were going to start out on an adventure. Well, it was actually going to be her adventure, only she needed their help.

Over the last few years, in fact since Mollie's wedding, they had all became friends and all because of two daughters, a coffee shop owner, and that freak storm they had been caught up in.

The three had become good friends, even though they were all very different types of women and of very different ages.

Alison now wondered if she was too old to do such a thing; the youngsters did this all the time, or so she had heard. Anyway Lisa and Margaret would soon be here and Alison was sure one of them could put her right.

Margaret had asked why she would want to do such a thing at her time of life and had asked if it was safe. Alison had since wondered this too.

She walked up to the table with the white plastic reserve card placed on it. She had laid the table out for three people who would perhaps turn her life around, in the love department that was.

Tucked up a corner they would sit well away from prying eyes and as long as they kept their voices low, no one would overhear their plotting.

She wouldn't place her laptop there just yet, in case someone had away with it, not that there were that many thieves in the area but better to be safe than sorry, as she had stuff on it; her stuff, business and personal.

Most people who came into her coffee shop she knew and trusted but there could always be just that one stranger who might steal.

The first person to pop in for a coffee latté that morning was Rosie; she had just finished the night shift at the hospital and was a regular. She had also been involved with this group of ladies since the time of the storm.

"In or take away, today?" Alison asked. "You look tired, Rosie; hard night?"

"Yes, as ever, it never slows down, but I do. I was going to retire and then thought better of it."

"Why was that?"

"I would miss the camaraderie of the staff and what would I do all day at home on my own?" Alison smiled at her and carried on making the coffee.

"I think perhaps I will have that coffee here," Rosie said.

"I'll bring it over. You go and sit down."

"Thanks."

Alison clicked the machine with the metal rod heating the milk in the silver coloured jug. The milk bubbled, spat and hissed before Alison poured it into a long glass mug.

Carrying it over to Rosie, Alison wondered if she should invite her to her little gathering. After all, she had never married either and was on her own at the moment and then she thought, perhaps not; Rosie was renowned as the hospital gossip. No one cared though because for all her gossiping, she was never spiteful and everyone loved her for her character and such a caring A and E nurse.

"There you go, enjoy," Alison said, standing the tall mug of latté down before her. "Perhaps a cake to go with the coffee," she suggested, knowing full well Rosie loved her sweet food, well actually any food come to that and she had the hips to show for it.

"No thanks; I had better not."

Surprised at Rosie's answer Alison went back to finish off her early morning tasks before Becky came in to work her few hours over midmorning to mid after-noon and then Mia came in after school hours until closing time.

Alison was watching the hands on the extra large round metal clock on the far wall. The girls would be in soon. They all called themselves girls but really two were middle age women and one quite a bit older; that was Margaret.

Alison still worried, if she was doing the right thing. Where would her adventure lead to? Who would it lead her to?

Well, too late now to cancel, it would soon be eleven o'clock and the keyboard send button would get pressed and she would be on her way.

"Hi Alison," Becky cheerfully said as she walked into work.

"Morning Becky," Alison replied.

Ten thirty already.

"What am I doing?" Alison thought and turned when she heard the ringing of the tiny brass bell above the door again. Shock horror, Margaret had arrived very early and was sure to try and talk her out of this quest of hers.

"Hello Margaret. Come on over. I've set the table in the corner."

It was really happening, Alison shivered at the thought.

"Morning, Alison," and Margaret went to sit down, speaking to Rosie as she passed her by. Rosie acknowledged Margaret with a smile and told her she was feeling tired and was going in a few minutes.

Another fifteen minutes passed and as Rosie's eye lids felt heavy, Alison's eyes were still following the clock's hands. She was still wondering if it was too late to pull out of this idea and then Lisa walked in.

"You okay Alison?" Lisa said as she walked closer to her and quickly noticed that she seemed a bit twitchy.

"Fine," Alison told her unconvincingly.

She made a pot of tea for Margaret and placed it on a silver tray with a small jug of proper milk, as Margaret always called whole milk. None of that old semi-skimmed rubbish, she would comment. No tea bags either. On the tray sat a tea strainer to catch those tea leaves as they flowed out with the brown boiling water into a china cup with saucer holding a silver spoon.

Margaret liked things done in the correct way, as she saw it, from her early years which had passed so quickly, she often said. Lisa loved her cappuccino with chocolate sprinkles on the top, in a large white cup which she could wrap her hands around, as did Alison. Modern day girls, they called themselves, even if they had just passed forty.

Carrying a white plate full of jam doughnuts, delivered by Danny earlier that morning along with the fresh bread, Alison now joined her two friends where they sat in the corner and she put the plate of calories down in front of them.

"How's Danny?" Margaret asked Alison.

Margaret knew Danny well enough, having lived just around the corner to his late wife when they were both young girls growing up.

"He's fine, as chatty as ever," Alison responded to Margaret.

"Now he's more your type and age, lost his wife ten or so years back, didn't he? Very sad, she was very young, you know but she probably trained him in her time." Margaret chuckled to herself as she said this. "I noticed last week when he arrived late, he smiled a lot at you."

"Oh, go on with you, he's not interested in me," Alison said.

"I wouldn't be so sure," Margaret said with a wicked glint in her eyes.

"Well let's get started then," Lisa said interrupting Margaret and her matchmaking, "where's your laptop Alison?"

"Oh! Yes, I'll go and get it." Alison was so nervous she had forgotten the one thing she needed to start off her adventure.

While Alison went for her laptop Margaret took a mouthful of doughnut and had red jam falling from one corner of her mouth but still she managed to remind Lisa that Danny had escorted Alison out more than once. Although Margaret wasn't sure if it was only for work reasons, meetings and such like.

"He does like her you know, she could do worse."

"Stop it, Margaret," Lisa said, smiling and shaking her head.

"Then again, she shouldn't be a man's slave and widowers usually want that from another wife," Margaret went on.

She had a poor opinion of men it seemed to Lisa, but she had also lost faith in men long ago due to her own circumstances.

"Life's deals make us think differently, sometimes." Lisa looked at Margaret and with a knowing smiled she wanted to say more but decided against it. Margaret remembered Lisa hadn't had an easy life either.

Today Margaret was there as support only. She

really didn't understand the reasoning behind Alison wanting to do this thing on a machine. It was all so very different in her time and to go looking for love on the internet at her time of life was madness and particularly since Alison had never been married before. Margaret felt she had no idea how some men could hold a woman's life back and also want so much from her at the same time.

She had lost her husband a few years before and was quite happy with her black and white cat, Patch, and her knitting, of course.

Rosie watched Alison return with her laptop. Her fascination with people's lives made her wonder what the three women huddled together, might be doing. She tried to eavesdrop on their conversation but was unable to and decided she really was too tired to care and needed her bed, after that busy nightshift.

"Bye all." She raised her hand to mark her leaving.

"Here goes nothing," Alison said as she opened up the program the three women had looked at last week.

Rosie just had to stretch her neck; she couldn't resist and caught a glimpse of the title on the laptop screen.

'Looking for Love'

Lisa didn't look up, just shouted bye to Rosie. The other two did the same because all three were engrossed in what was on the screen.

Alison, with the help of her two friends had filled in the relevant details last week. Lisa, who was the youngest of the three, had known more about these different sites because of hearing her young daughter and her friends talking. Not that Beth ever used them as she'd had Andy as a boyfriend since her school years.

It was Lisa who had encouraged Alison, after she had made it quite clear, that was what she wanted.

Lisa had never felt the need to go looking for love, having been let down many, many years before with a man she loved deeply, a man she never really ever got over, a man who ran out on her and after only two years of marriage, leaving her with their two year old daughter, Beth.

Lisa had never looked again.

So Alison's dating line was open, the tiny red hearts had drifted over the page before her details appeared. Had anyone replied?

Chapter Two
E-mails

A written profile showed, giving information on a man in his late forties. Yes a match had been made. His name was Philip but he liked to be known as Phil. He had worked on cruise ships and travelled the world. He also wrote that it would be good to have a companion who was interested in travelling, to go with him and explore the places he had seen.

"He's a show off," Margaret said straight away.

"He might do any number of jobs on board, from waiter to cabin boy," Lisa remarked. They all laughed.

"Bit old for a cabin boy," Alison said and added he could be the captain.

"Would you have time to go traipsing around the world and leave your coffee shop?" Margaret then asked with an underlying tone.

The other two rolled their eyes at each other and said nothing as Margaret took another bite out of her doughnut.

He liked dogs and cats and had a daughter of twenty five, who didn't live with him.

"Well that's one good point, he likes cats," Margaret commented between her mouthfuls of the quickly disappearing doughnut.

There was little more for the women to read and Margaret had lost interest as the other two scrolled down over more men's profiles. They returned to

Philip's page.

The city he lived in was Southampton, he wrote.

Alison knew the area well from her younger years when a student there and when she went to the docks to see which ships were in port, a fascination of hers at the time.

"You have that in common then," Lisa said.

His actual address he left off. No home phone number or mobile phone number but there was an e-mail address.

"Go on then, e-mail him," Lisa egged Alison on.

"Why don't you just go to Southampton and spend the day walking around with a board held up high, like the people do at the airports." Margaret was being sarcastic as she thought it all such a waste of time. "If you were destined to marry, you would have found someone by now. Grow up. You missed the boat; like the pun?" She grinned. "Be like me, get a cat."

Margaret had no understanding of people and their needs. She hadn't had a happy marriage and other than the money coming in, which she now missed and the company that perhaps she wanted, no other man was getting into her life ever again.

Yes she was lonely, sometimes, now that her daughter Mollie had married and moved away and still she hadn't given her grandchildren. 'Selfish girl, always was, don't know why father doted on her,' this often crossed her mind. Margaret muttered the words under her breath once and Mollie had overheard her mother's cruel words.

Mollie should have known; mother and daughter

had never been close.

Lisa and Alison sometimes wondered how the three of them ever became friends. Margaret could be quite cutting with her words sometimes and mostly showed a hard exterior but just a few people had been privileged to see her marshmallow insides, Lisa being one of them.

Both Lisa and Alison wondered what had happened in Margaret's life to make her so sour. Although they met up with Margaret quite often, she had only spilled a little of her life's history to them.

"I'm off. See you next week for coffee, usual time?" Margaret said as stood to leave.

"See you next week," Alison and Lisa said together.

Little did the three women know then there wouldn't be a next week's meeting in this coffee shop.

"Right let's get this arranged," Lisa said, feeling quite pleased Margaret had left them to it.

"Oh I don't know, should I?" Alison was having a wobble.

She wanted to know where she should meet an unknown man.

"Don't jump the gun. Talk to him via e-mail, until you feel you want to meet and ask for a picture. You might hate the look of him." Lisa now helped herself to a doughnut.

"What if he turns out to be an axe murderer?" Alison said. She was scaring herself now.

She had never done anything like this before, to go and meet a complete stranger. Was she being foolish?

"Oh come on, really? Of course he's not an axe murderer," Lisa said licking her fingers clear of sugar.

"But how do you know? You hear of these things on the news all the time." Alison was getting nervous again. When she worried she got twitchy and fiddled with all her dress rings, Lisa had noticed this before. Her fingers on her right hand were all covered in white gold rings, some fancy, others with stones, but on her left fingers, there were none. She kept all those fingers empty for a reason, no man could be mistaken, *she was not married*.

She may have light grey hair but that had come about when she was very young, through illness and she had never coloured it.

"Look Alison, arrange a meet up point, in a bar of a hotel or a nice restaurant. Somewhere where there are lots of people visiting and working, a safe place."

Lisa told her she would go with her, if she wanted her too. To sit across the room and just watch, even keep guard.

Alison went quiet for a while. She was thinking hard about all this.

"Okay what shall I write?" She asked Lisa.

"Come on; I can't do it all for you. I'm off to the toilet, I've jam all over my fingers; you start writing."

Alison began, one word typed and she immediately went blank, her fingers hanging above the keys as Lisa returned.

"Is that all you have written? Hello! Perhaps you should sleep on it. Phone me tomorrow. I have to go now, Beth and Andy are returning from the hospital this after-noon with my new grandson and they said they would be popping in."

Lisa stood to leave and Alison stood too, to give her friend a hug and thank her.

She was a little envious of Lisa being a grandmother but then she knew you needed your own children to become a granny and now it was too late for her, or so she thought, at forty.

Becky called over. Alison hadn't realised the time had gone so quickly.

"I'm off now, Joe's here to give me a lift."

"Okay, bye Becky."

The rest of the afternoon went slowly as Mondays often did. Alison clicked onto her page where she entered her takings and brought up other pages connected with the coffee shop. Up to date, it hadn't been a bad year and now the summer had arrived there would be more tourists.

She was about to close down her laptop but her fingers still hovered over the keys. She was remembering that site, *'Looking for Love'*. Should she take another look? She took a deep breath and clicked, the page opened again with those ridiculous falling red hearts floating across the screen, then she saw Phil had added his photo.

Even as a reserved woman of her age, she said *'wow'* aloud and then felt stupid and looked around to see if anyone had heard and was watching her, as though they would have read her mind if they had been.

Holding her chest she was relieved to see no one else had come in and the few people left in her shop were either talking or, as the one man over by the window had his head buried in his newspaper which was folded back to the sports page.

'Oh, this Phil person is rather handsome, in a distinguished way,' she commented quietly to herself having turned her eyes back to the laptop.

There was a little grey at the sides of his dark hair and a lovely smile came from both mouth and blue eyes. From what she could see he wore a shirt and tie with a dark blue waistcoat. Smart, she thought. Yet there was something about his looks, he seemed familiar to her. Was it that dimple in one cheek that reminded her of someone? Had she seen him before somewhere?

She closed the site and decided to shut up shop as the last man, the one with the newspaper folded and tucked under his arm, stood to leave.

"Bye," she said.

He left with a slight nod of his head towards her.

She followed him over to the door. Locking it behind him and turning the sign to CLOSED she told Mia she could leave early that day.

Alison turned the lights out, covered the cups and mugs with a clean tea towel and made sure the glass cake stands had their covers in place.

Alison lived above the coffee shop and that's where she headed, to slouch out on her sofa with a ping dinner. She found a few in her freezer and chose a beef curry, placed it in the micro-wave; ten minutes passed by before the machine went ping.

Settled on her grey comfy sofa with a mixture of grey and pink cushions supporting her back, she watched the news and ate her dinner from a bowl. Boring news she thought and began flicking channels. Watched a bit of this and that but couldn't settle into anything.

Margaret had told her, she wouldn't get to hold the TV control, if she had a man in her life.

Finishing her dinner she laid the bowl down on the floor and picked up her i-pad. He was on line. A green dot showed her he was on messenger too. How did that happen? She wished she understood the internet better. She must have touched a button, she frowned. Files and things to do with her business were not a problem to her, but the rest; well she hadn't been interested enough in this thing called the web, to learn.

What should she write?

Taking hold of her laptop now, she firmly wedged it on her own lap. She fiddled with her shoulder length hair, now hanging loose from its bun. The bun she always wore on the top of her head while working.

Unwittingly she had been itching to go back all evening to that site, '*Looking for love.*' She wanted another look at the handsome man on her laptop.

Why she tidied her hair or pulled her pyjama jacket straight, she didn't know, because he wasn't going to see her, was he? Face time wasn't something Alison had ever done. But she had to feel right and now she was ready and clicked the keys.

'Hello,' she wrote.

'Hello back,' he wrote.

Now what should she do or write? She decided

just to write what she had been doing that day. Who she had met, but only write their first names, and then asked him what his day had been like. Yes, that's okay she thought, keep it simple, she hadn't given too much away. She was being careful, just in case he was an axe murderer. She pressed the key; sent.

Alison waited; nothing. She sighed and headed off to the bathroom. She had hardly started brushing her teeth when she heard the ping sound on her i-pad. She wondered if that could be him but carried on finishing her bathroom routine. I'll make him wait. Oh dear, she was acting like a teenager again, she thought, as the face cream went on. That cream reminded her, she was no teenager.

She snuggled up on the sofa once more, picked up her i-pad this time and opened it. It was him. What, how did he do that? She was still unsure of this technology, having only recently bought an i-pad. She opened his message.

He had returned with his day's information and it was quite ordinary, just like her's really. He had finished some drawings of an indoor shopping centre which he had been working on for months and he was pleased with the outcome.

Margaret said he was a show off; "he is pleased with his own work," she said aloud and smirked.

He worked on a cruise ship, he had said. Was he lying to her or was she just trying not to like him? Looking for faults? A reason not to do this, Alison wondered at herself, but he was handsome.

They both said their goodnights and both machines were shut down.

Alison knew she had to phone Lisa first thing tomorrow with the outcome of hers and Phil's connection that night. She needed her opinion and wanted to show her how good looking he was and Alison sighed as she closed her eyes to dream.

Could she at last be on the road to finding a man to love and him to love her?

Chapter Three
The Photograph

Alison was up bright and early and the first thing she had to do was not phone Lisa but to open her laptop, quickly followed by her i-pad. There was disappointment waiting for her. No messages on either. She checked her laptop e-mails again as though they would be different to her i-pad, but nothing. Her heart sank. The urgency she'd had last night to phone Lisa had subsided.

She didn't fancy breakfast and once she was dressed and ready for work she went down to the shop. Tidying around she stopped and sat on one of the tall metal stools at the central counter and stared into space, her mind wandering. She took a lemon cup cake from under the glass dome and nibbled at it, she didn't really want it. Before long she had made herself a coffee, black and strong this time; she needed that to pull herself together and concentrate on work and not keep checking to see if Phil had left her a message. She was no teenager, she had established that and yet she felt like one again. Did she want this? She phoned Lisa now.

"Hi, I must see you, can you come over. I have a photo," she said, hardly giving Lisa the time to say hello.

***

Lisa had been tossing and turning all night after hearing the name Phil; was it just a coincidence? Yes of course it was; she told herself. Lots of men are called Phil. But still she had slept badly because of that name, his name, that of a young boy she had courted in school and then married while so young and who was the father of her daughter, Beth.

He was named Philip but asked everyone to call him Phil.

Lisa had never loved anyone since Phil. He had been her everything and from such a young age.

When she found herself pregnant and only just eighteen she had been forced to marry him, not that she had seen that as a hardship.

It was her parents who worried what people in their village would say and it was them that had made the couple move away.

The marriage had only lasted two years after that forced move, a move from where she had been brought up, where she had friends. Here she had known no one and had no friends to support her with a first baby. To make matters worse she had no mother's help either, in fact she didn't even visit Lisa or her grandchild ever again.

Lisa had found it hard to cope with a baby, a new place to live and she felt so desperately alone and with little money coming in things hadn't been great but still she adored Beth and Phil.

When Phil arrived home from work each night she did nothing but moan or cry at him. He was only a few months older than her. Neither Phil nor Lisa could manage and even now she made excuses in her mind for him leaving.

They had been too young, she would say to anyone who asked, not that many people did.

***

"I'll be right over," Lisa told Alison.

An hour went by and Alison was feeling twitchy again. Where was Lisa? She was about to phone her again when the little brass door bell overhead tinkled and Lisa walked in.

"Hi." Lisa walked up to the coffee counter where Becky made her a skinny latté.

Alison smiled at Lisa and nodded to point her towards a table close by the open window, she would join her there.

The shop was very busy that lunch time and Alison was finding it hard to get away to find the time to sit with Lisa. She had almost finished her coffee by the time Alison managed to sit down with her.

"Sorry about that but I couldn't leave Becky on her own, it's been a crazy morning. Anyway I have his photo."

Alison opened her laptop and signed on to '*Looking for love'*. The red hearts did their usual thing and floated over the page, before she could bring his photo up. She twisted the laptop around so Lisa could see him. She looked hard at his profile.

"Isn't he handsome?" Alison said with a huge grin on her face.

Lisa didn't answer. She went pale and felt cold with goose bumps showing on her arms, where her top didn't reach her wrists. Her heart felt like a knife had been pushed in and then twisted.

"Well, what do you think?" Alison still excited, before the disappointment came because Lisa hadn't jumped up and down in agreement.

"I have to go," Lisa said, as she jumped from her chair.

Shaking inside she quickly walked out, pushing through a group of office workers coming in for a late lunch, as they often did. She didn't apologise. They thought her rather rude but made no comment as they found a table.

Alison had been left in limbo as she watched Lisa leave. She had no idea what she had said or done to upset her friend, to make her leave so suddenly and without a word spoken.

Alison had no chance of running after her; the office workers needed serving and Becky was already run off her feet. Alison had to stop and help her. She had watched Lisa dash to her car though and drive off at speed; that was so unlike her. Lisa had always made it clear she was worried about getting a speeding ticket. In fact, the thought of being on the wrong side of the law, frightened her. This was only one of her hidden problems which she carried from having had such a strict father who marched around his home, holding a bible in his hand and waving it at Lisa whenever he told her off for something perhaps she hadn't even done.

Alison and Margaret were the only two people to know Lisa had been a scared little girl when growing up and that during her adult life this had caused her to suffer with anxiety and even depression on occasions, possibly post natal depression too.

It was a depression not recognised so much back when she gave birth to Beth, but she had since thought about it, because that, in itself would have been difficult for Phil to cope with, well perhaps any man; again Lisa forgave the man she loved and blamed herself.

Neither of her friends knew her then and wished they had, to have helped her.

Lisa had to pull into a lay-by and catch her breath. She threw her head back to lie on the headrest and shut her eyes, to think. All her past came flooding back: childhood, parents, schooling, moving, Beth and her, Phil. He had always been good to her, kind and protective, loved her when others didn't.

She leant forward over the car's steering wheel, covered her eyes and cried.

Surely not. Not, after all these years. It couldn't be him. Her first and only love; the young boy turned man who gave her courage to grow. Things kept repeating themselves in her head.

He had aged, yes, but then so had she. He still had those same wonderful blue sparkling eyes and the mouth she had kissed with pleasure. The one dimple in his left cheek showed, just like his daughter's and now his granddaughter's.

Why? After all this time, why did he have to come back and perhaps into her friend's life, not hers?

Here, where she would most possibly bump into him, time and time again. What was she going to do?

Her mobile phone rang, making her jump. Her nerves were on edge again. She had to be watchful after she had been placed on HRT a few years back when Beth had made her go to the doctor. She couldn't help her body, it was the way some women were made, the doctor explained.

When she looked at her phone, she saw it was Alison and turned it off. Not now, she thought, she couldn't talk to her right now, perhaps later.

Lisa eventually arrived home, pulled into her car space outside the terraced house she had lived in for twenty five years now. It would have belonged to her, if he had stayed and paid a mortgage, but no, she had had to pay rent on the building.

Barney came trotting up to her as she opened the door. He was an old dog but his Labrador's black coat was still shiny and he loved to rub it around her legs before he tried to jump up and lick her face.

"Hello, old boy." Lisa made him sit before she bent down to rub him. He had made such a difference to her life over the past five years and now with her arms about his neck, she cried some more. She didn't expect that again.

Was it because she didn't know how much longer she would have Barney? He had been poorly; she had been backwards and forwards to the vet recently, spent a small fortune on him but she didn't care. Was it Barney that made her cry, or was it Phil?

She made her way into the kitchen and put the kettle on. She made herself a mug of tea and sat down in the sitting room, all in a very automatic way.

She found her tea cold, when she put her lips to

the mug sometime later.

Sitting on her sofa she had again laid her head back and daydreamed of her old life and how time had slipped by, as it had that afternoon.

How different her life could have been.

What was she going to say to Alison, who seemed so smitten with this man in the photo? Should she try to put her off of him? Tell her to give it all up or tell her who he really was? Tell her he was still married, and to her! But then Beth might find out.

She would have to sleep on it. She yawned, she felt emotionally exhausted but the evening was still young.

Her home phone rang, she wouldn't answer it. She couldn't answer it. A message was being left.

"Hi mum, have you time to pop over. Baby has a high temperature. Sorry to bother you," and Lisa had grabbed the phone before it rang off and had told her daughter she would be there within the half hour.

Chapter Four
Love

Lisa arrived at Beth's house and was greeted by a daughter with a newborn screaming in her arms and a three year old toddler hanging onto her jeans.

"Hello my darlings," Lisa said to the family she adored.

Taking baby from Beth's arms, she kissed her daughter and smiled, telling her to put the kettle on.

English tea made everything seem better, even now in this modern day of so much coffee.

"What's up little boy?" Lisa said while rocking him in her arms and beaming down at him. She needed a distraction from that photo and she had it, here with her grandchildren.

"Now sit down and enjoy a cupper and pass me the thermometer," she said to Beth.

"Oh mum, we don't have thermometers anymore. Here stick this on his forehead."

Lisa felt old fashioned at that very moment and remembered back to when she held Beth dressed all in white in her arms and how soon after Phil had left her. She had cried bucket loads of tears back then just as she had only an hour or so ago.

She had had to be strong over all those years while bringing up Beth. She had battled and fought off her insecurities and succeeded. So why couldn't she get this man out of her head now?

Beth noticed her mother's frown.

"Is baby really poorly?"

"Oh! No dear, sorry. I was miles away, thinking about something else."

"Can I help?"

"No I'll be fine. Now come on, you're a nurse; this baby is just too hot with all these clothes on. Get the denim trousers off and let some air around him," Lisa told her daughter.

They spent what was left of the day together and Lisa had great fun playing with her granddaughter while Beth took a nap when baby did.

Lisa had buried her phone in the bottom of her bag and had turned it on to silent, thinking there was no way she was going to answer it or bother to look for it. This was just as well as Lily kept on chatting to her grandma about the baby and how it had no name and was too small to play with and she wanted grandma to play. Lisa laughed as she carried on dressing dolls with Lily.

Lisa asked Beth when she reappeared why baby had no name yet. Beth told her she and Andy couldn't agree on one and felt there was no hurry. They were also trying to involve their little girl, in choosing a name.

"And a wedding date, dare I ask?"

"Oh mum, you know we don't care about a bit of paper," Beth said while looking down at Lily who was jumping around and dancing in a Snow White play dress now instead of a pair of pyjamas which she had been told to put on an age ago, to be ready to go to bed.

"I'm a princess; I want to be a pretty bridesmaid."

Lily could talk well for a three year old.

"I know, one day, perhaps." Beth took Lily by the hand and kissed it as she curtsied for her mother.

Playtime always warmed Lisa's heart and she smiled away her hidden tears as she watched her two girls.

Baby was settled now and Lily was tucked up in bed. Andy was working late again even though he should have been on leave with this new baby and its mother.

Lisa worried but said nothing; she wouldn't be an interfering mother but wanted to give the support she had never been given.

Lisa had a good understanding with Beth now their relationship had repaired itself after Beth's teenage years and she knew she could go to her mother at any time. Such a different relationship to the one they had when Beth was still at school and going out with Andy who was that much older and already out to work.

Lisa had worried when Beth first met Andy and she had tried to stop her seeing him. Was history going to repeat itself? It hadn't and Lisa was happy enough now, only she wished they were married and that baby had a name.

But Lisa had learned from experience that children change, they grow into adults, yet still most mothers worry about their offspring whatever their age and Lisa had wanted to protect Beth back then as she did now.

She needed to talk to her about her father in case he was in the area, but this was not the moment;

perhaps another day.

"Mum, what's worrying you?"

"Nothing, honestly, I'll be fine. It's just a blast from the past that hit me today. It's nothing for you to concern yourself about. Well, I'd better be off, Barney will be missing me." She used him as her excuse to leave.

"How is he?"

"Old, bless him."

Lisa left her daughter to have an early night, knowing she would be up very soon to feed baby. She hoped Andy would be home soon and take a few days off work, to support her daughter.

Just a small niggling thought crossed Lisa's mind; was he really at work? Yes of course he was. He adored his little family and more so Beth, she assured herself.

Lisa arrived home and soon found herself sitting in the middle of her floor surrounded by photos going back some thirty or forty years. Some were even black and white.

There were photos of her parents, a strong controlling mother but timid around her husband, the father who quoted the bible to his children. Her siblings, who she hadn't seen since she was sent away that day and they all stared back at her, reminding her.

After all, she had been a mistake; her father had told her on many occasions. She was ten years older than her nearest sister who was only eight at the time she left home; there had been two more children, a boy and another baby girl. She suddenly wondered what had happened to them. What had their lives been like?

And then there were so many photos of her and Phil together. A few at school, another when she had that baby bump. At that point she kicked the box across the floor; she couldn't look at any more.

So she stretched out on the sofa and fell asleep with Barney next to her.

Chapter Five
Gas

Lisa couldn't put Alison off any longer and with a heavy heart she drove to the coffee shop.

"Hi, time for coffee," Lisa said as she walked through the door.

Alison stopped what she was doing and looked up on hearing Lisa's voice. She walked around from her side of the coffee counter to greet her. They hugged and Lisa apologised for suddenly leaving yesterday. She said she had felt unwell and just had to go but she was fine again now.

"So come on; tell me what's happening," Lisa asked, curbing her inner feelings.

"You look very red eyed and tired: are you sure you're all right?" Alison asked.

"I'm fine. I was up late last night." In fact she hadn't reached her bed. She had slept on her sofa.

Lisa had decided not to say she knew this man, Phil. It would have opened up so many old wounds and there would be too much to explain and really Lisa couldn't handle talking about it all. And there was Beth to think of too; if the information got out before she had time to explain, what then?

The two women sat and drank their coffee together. Alison talked of her e-mails with Phil and that they were going well, back and forth. She felt they would be meeting very soon.

"So, you like him, then?" Lisa asked, half hoping

she wouldn't.

"Well, yes. He sounds okay, if I can believe all he writes," Alison replied, still unsure of him.

"Umm," was all Lisa could mumble.

"Is there a problem?" Alison asked.

"No, just don't rush it. There could be more men out there to meet."

"I know. How about a cup cake? Look, Rosie is on her way in and she will join us." Alison had suddenly felt very awkward in her friend's company.

"Hi Rosie, over here," and Alison waved at her to join them. Immediately Rosie thought she might be able to gain some information about why they were looking at a dating site the other day, when she was last in.

Which one of the three women was interested in finding a man? She really couldn't guess.

"What's happening then? I hear you're a grandmother again Lisa. I saw the baby in the hospital baby unit. Isn't he a dear?" Rosie was trying to work her way around to love stories and asked if wedding bells would chime soon.

"We could do with another lovely wedding. It's been five years now, since Mollie's. Do you know anyone heading up the aisle?"

"No; do you Lisa?" Alison said as her business phone rang and she walked off to answer it.

Alison felt relief at the ringing tone.

"Come on Lisa. I saw that laptop site the other day and it can't possibly be Margaret who's looking. *Looking for love.*"

Lisa couldn't hide her wet eyes and shrugged.

"You, okay, you don't look so good?" Rosie wondered if it was Lisa who had found love and lost it.

"Yes, just very tired," Lisa replied.

Becky called over to Alison as she replaced the phone on its holder.

"This gas keeps going out," Becky complained.

"I have the gas man coming out next week. It was doing that on and off thing, when you were on holiday last week. Monday is the earliest he can come out. He said it must just be a switch not connecting properly. As long as there's no smell of gas we're okay. Just turn it off and on again, it will work," Alison told her.

"Okay." The oven was back on and waiting for the cake mixture to go in.

Rosie had to leave for her late afternoon/evening shift, without gaining the knowledge of who was looking for love. She thought she would have to try another day; Rosie wouldn't let it rest until she knew. But she had ruled out Margaret.

"Well I'll be off too," Lisa said. "Hope the gas stays on. Bye."

"See you, Lisa. Bye," Alison shouted from where she was placing another tray of cup cakes into a warm oven.

The first batch smelled delicious while cooling on their wire rack.

"There seems to be a problem with the oven door not shutting," Becky said and pointed to the oven.

"Yes, perhaps that's why the gas flames keep going out," Alison said and tried closing the door again. There was a click, as though it had caught but as Alison turned her back it slowly drifted open just a whisker.

"I think I'll ring that gas man again," and she did just that, only to be told the same.

As long as there is no gas smell, he will be out next Monday at nine a.m. as arranged.

"Well I can't do any more, Becky. You go home. I'm going to close up early as Mia can't come in today after school.

"Are you sure?" Becky asked.

"Yes; you go. We're not busy."

The last few customers left and Alison turned the sign on the door over to CLOSED.

She headed off upstairs to find her laptop. Halfway up, she stopped to wonder what she was doing, shutting up shop early and losing money, just so she could go online to find a man without disturbance.

Margaret would say she was wasting her time; perhaps she was right. Alison was having second thoughts about Phil or even finding any man come to that.

She decided to make herself a proper dinner that evening. Normally she would be in a rush to eat after working long hours in the shop and just grab a box dinner.

Burying herself in her cooking would stop her having time to worry about e-mails coming from a certain man. Well that was her thinking, but it never happened. Why had she ever started with all of this? Her mind was a whirl like her hand stirring the pot on the gas hob. Her mind kept wandering back to *Love,* films with happy endings and books, she enjoyed them all.

She pushed the wooden spoon around in the Bolognese mixture which she had prepared with extra mushrooms. The water was on for the spaghetti but still it wasn't boiling.

"That damned gas has gone out up here now," she moaned under her breath. Turning the knob she clicked the gas off and on again. It ignited. "Thank you! Now, can I cook?"

She was talking to a gas ring, now. Things were getting bad.

While the water boiled she rushed downstairs to save the cupcakes from burning. She had forgotten them until the gorgeous smell wafted up the stairs to reach her nose.

Oh, this love thing is doing me no good, nor my business, she told herself.

She reached the cakes just in time before any overcooking browned their tops. She pulled them from the oven, which had gone off again.

She placed the cakes onto a cooling tray and looked them over. She knew the cream icing would cover any flaws.

Walking back upstairs, she wondered about the gas which had gone off downstairs and had actually saved her cakes from totally burning.

Thankful her dinner was cooked when she reached it.

Eventually she was eating in front of the TV, but her eyes kept drifting over to her laptop. It was no good; as the last mouthful disappeared from her bowl, the laptop was on her lap.

The site was open and there he was, smiling at her.

"Good day," he wrote.

"Not really," she wrote back. "Trouble with the gas."

Then she waffled on about her problems and cooking cupcakes and dinner. She wondered if he would be bored with her chatter and would stop writing to her. But he said he had had a few issues as well himself that day and soon they were writing back and forth to each other, as if they had known each other forever.

When Alison finally said goodnight she felt pleased and not so silly. Then a shock thought turned her insides over; what had she done? Only arranged a meeting for Sunday, the only day when she would normally shut up early at four in the afternoon and he was to join her here, in her coffee shop, where she lived. What had she been thinking?

Panic set in. She had given him her address. She shouldn't have done that. Lisa! She had to phone Lisa.

Alison was on the phone and pacing up and down her flat. Cooking smells lingered in the air, from dinner and the cakes.

"Come on; answer," she said as if Lisa would hear. "Hurry up."

Lisa was out. Alison left a message.

"I will try her mobile phone," she was talking to herself again and she frowned and still she was pacing.

Lisa's phone rang and rang, then went to voice mail. Alison left another message and then threw the phone across the sofa. She thought she might try the i-pad, but of course Lisa never took hers out the house, did she? Alison knew that. She left written words on messenger anyway. One way or another Alison would talk to Lisa before the night was out, she hoped.

Chapter Six
Change of Events

Lisa was visiting Beth and her grandchildren. She was helping with baths and getting very wet from a giggling granddaughter, who thought it was great fun to splash her grandma. Bedtime stories came next and Lily quietened down.

Andy was going to be home late, again, which would give Lisa the chance to gently bring up the subject of where he was.

"Mum, don't worry yourself," said Beth. "He's up for promotion and needs to be seen to be doing. He wants to get on."

"That's all well and good, but you're here with a little one and a new baby."

"We're fine. It's just bad timing. Can't you see how happy I am?"

Beth loved her mum and understood her, so was polite; if it had been anyone else interfering she would have had something to say.

Lisa could see Beth was happy, but still she worried. Beth's father had left her and Lisa couldn't forget all the hard years.

The evening went easily by, mother and daughter chatted until gone ten when Andy walked in with a man bag slung over his shoulder, from where papers poked out next to his laptop.

"Hi," he said to Lisa and walked straight over to Beth and kissed her cheek, asked after his babies and flopped into an armchair.

"I'll be off home. Love you all." Lisa left and headed home, feeling more content that her daughter was happy and in love.

When she walked into her home she noticed the red button flashing on the answer phone. A message; she played it. The time was just gone eleven, too late to return Alison's phone call. Lisa was still trying to avoid the question of Phil.

The morning came and both Lisa and Alison had spent the night tossing and turning, both thinking of the same man but with very different reasons.

Lisa's phone rang as she walked down the stairs. Barney was sitting waiting for her as she opened the kitchen door.

"Morning old boy, how are you today?" and she ruffled his head. Barney licked her hand.

Should she get the phone? She knew she should, but hesitated. Just as she picked up the receiver it rang off and went to answer mode.

"It's me; whatever am I going to do?"

And with that there was a massive explosion.

Oh, my God! Lisa knew it was Alison. Whatever had happened? She had to get over there. But first she dialled 999, asked for ambulance and fire and explained what she had heard after giving Alison's address. Before she could think clearly she was in her day clothes, in her car and on the road. Heading for the coffee shop, her mind was racing, as was her car.

It took her less than the usual half an hour to get there. Speed limits never crossed her mind that day. She was aware to take care though, but it was early and not too much traffic was about.

On arriving at the coffee shop it looked like a war zone to her, not that she had ever been in a war zone, but she, like most people had seen those dreadful places on the news programs.

Lisa covered her lower face with her hand, to mask her open mouth and the scream which was leaving it.

There was only half a coffee shop still standing.

***

Margaret never slept well these days, since losing her husband and Mollie moving out; or was it an age thing? Margaret didn't really know, perhaps a mix of all. Anyway, she had been up early and living nearer to the coffee shop she had heard the bang. When she looked out of her window, she had seen large curls of smoke rising. She turned on the radio and there was a woman's voice reading out a newsflash.

'Coffee shop explodes!'

That was all Margaret took in. She had to get down there as soon as she could and check on Alison.

When she pulled around the corner in her car there was a road block. She, like many others parked and walked the few hundred yards to have a better look. Many knew Alison and used her coffee shop at least once a week.

Margaret saw Lisa at the front of a small group of people talking to a policeman. Margaret pushed her way through and touched Lisa's arm.

"Oh Margaret, I'm so glad you came."

"Alison, is she in there?"

"Yes, we think so," and Lisa told Margaret about her phone call.

"The firemen are in there, trying to find her," Lisa explained.

More and more people were turning up. Gossip was spreading within the crowd.

"It was a gas explosion, you know."

"Really?"

"Was anyone hurt?" people were asking.

Speculation was coming from the worried voices all around and quickly circulated.

Lisa and Margaret waited and suddenly a cheer went up. The firemen had found someone. Two firemen appeared holding someone who could barely walk between them.

"It's a man," Lisa said. "It's Danny, the bread and doughnut delivery man."

"What about Alison?" Margaret screamed at another fireman.

"We're going back in," he said.

Two different firemen went rushing in, breathing equipment strapped on their backs. It was only minutes later when they returned carrying a body wrapped in a blanket.

"No!" Lisa gasped. "Is she dead?"

Margaret watched and saw a paramedic running with a stretcher. The body was placed on this, then two paramedics were leaning over it.

Was the body Alison's? Was she alive? The whole crowd was deadly quiet now. Then a roar went up, *yes alive*.

The siren sounded and the ambulance took off at speed. A policewoman turned to Lisa and told her, it was her friend, Alison. This policewoman had, over the years, also popped in for a coffee.

"Let's get to the hospital," Lisa said, turning to Margaret. "Where are you parked?"

"In a side street, back there," she answered. "You?"

"Over there and I'm boxed in." Lisa pointed to her car.

She had been one of the first to arrive on the scene.

"Okay we'll take my car," Margaret said and they both ran; well, Margaret perhaps did a quick walk to get back to her car and then both headed off to the hospital.

On arriving, Rosie dashed forward to greet both Lisa and Margaret in A and E.

"Alison is in with the burns specialists right now," Rosie told them.

"Well how is she?" a concerned Lisa asked. She was feeling rather dizzy with the shock of hearing Alison's voice followed by that explosion.

"Poorly. Not so much with her burns but her head wound. She is waiting on a scan."

"Is that all you can tell us?" Margaret took up the questioning; she could see Lisa was a bit shaky, to say the least.

"Go and get a coffee, the pair of you. It will be a while before we know much. I'll come and find you when we know more. Okay?" Rosie hugged them both and returned to her work in A and E.

Reluctantly Lisa went with Margaret to find a coffee machine and a seat. Both women were quiet for some time and then slowly they began to converse.

There was one strange thing Margaret had noticed and wanted to discuss with Lisa.

"Did you see that tall, rather distinguished looking man asking questions of the policeman?" Margaret enquired of Lisa.

"No," Lisa snapped. She was sensitive just now.

"He was standing close by the tape surrounding the rubble. I watched him push his way to the front of the crowd, Lisa."

"No, who was he?" Lisa asked.

"I don't know, thought you might."

"A reporter, perhaps," Lisa suggested.

"No I don't think so. He said Alison's name before anyone had told him."

"Are you sure? Maybe he had been in for coffee sometime; what did he look like?" Lisa asked.

Margaret seemed to describe the man in the photo on Alison's laptop, on the love site. But she hadn't seen that photo. She thought better than to tell Margaret who she thought he might be because she was still hoping it wasn't Phil.

The women waited, two hours went by and Lisa decided to phone her daughter. She must have heard the news by now. In her rush to get to Alison, Lisa hadn't picked up her bag with her mobile phone in.

"Here use mine," Margaret passed her a small white thing which Lisa looked at in a strange sort of way.

"I know, it's old and out of date, but I only carry it for emergencies, like if I break down."

Lisa and Beth had a short conversation before Rosie appeared and interrupted them. Lisa told her daughter she had to go and would phone her later.

Rosie's news on Alison's condition was mixed. She wasn't badly burnt as she had been found just inside the doorway of the bathroom which in some way had protected her from the gas cooker that exploded downstairs, shooting out its flames. That's what Jack the paramedic had said anyway and the way Danny had covered himself and fell on top of her all helped.

Only she had been knocked out from a head injury which was now cause for alarm. Rosie told both Lisa and Margaret to go home, get some rest and come back tomorrow.

The day had flown by, yet it had seemed to drag on, too. A strange thing, Lisa thought as Margaret drove her home. Neither woman spoke. Lisa had so much floating around in her head and her face showed the strain.

Margaret expressed to Lisa that she looked as though she needed to rest, that the shock of hearing the explosion on the other end of her phone would have shaken anyone up. A nice cup of tea and a sleep would do her the world of good, even if it wasn't night time.

Margaret suddenly remembered Danny, as she pulled up outside Lisa's house.

"Lisa we never asked about Danny."

"Oh no, we should have; we will tomorrow."

It had been Danny who the fire crew pulled from the rubble first but he hadn't been the two women's priority.

Margaret settled Lisa with a milky hot chocolate, instead of tea and made sure she was all right before leaving her.

"I'll pop by tomorrow and pick you up; we can go and collect your car. Okay? Then we'll go to the hospital. Bye." And Margaret left.

Barney lay on the rug next to the sofa at Lisa's feet, while she just stared at the blank screen of the TV. It had all been too much for her that day.

Chapter Seven
Remembering

Lisa snuggled down on her sofa with a brown velour throw loosely around her. She couldn't bring herself to go to bed; it was just too much effort.

It was to be a long evening and night, she couldn't sleep. Yet she must have drifted in and out of dreams, for every time she closed her eyes Phil came to her.

Pictures of Phil were playing on her mind. There they were, hiding around corners of the school buildings at break time, snatching a kiss or two before the teachers caught them. She didn't know it, but she was tossing and turning on her sofa.

Their plans for the future were often talked about as they sat together on the school playing fields at lunch time and as restless as she was in that time, she was now restless in this time. She woke imagining she heard their words before turning over and nodding off again.

Phil was walking her home, leaving her just before her house, so she didn't get seen by her mother.

Then the day she found out she was to have his baby, their Beth, caused another sudden awakening accompanied by a groan this time before sleep came once again.

Now Lisa's parents came rushing back into her dreams and they were pushing through a wedding, in which neither she or Phil had any say. Her parents arranged for her and Phil to move away to this house where she still lived. They had no choice in that either. Everything came flooding back and oh, how she remembered his kisses, they had melted her heart.

In her dreams she could almost feel his school boy arms wrapped around her, a contented moan came from her smiling lips. Those thin arms turned into the arms of a man with strong muscles. She could almost feel his strength and the warmth wrapping around her as she slept. She missed those arms and woke with another start finding her own arms and blanket wrapped tightly around her body.

She missed him; where was he? For a split second she didn't know where she was.

"What's the time?" she asked herself, while rubbing at her eyes and sitting herself up to lean over and look to the clock. She was surprised, 9 am. She had overslept. Margaret would soon be here. Lisa knew she had to phone her right away, but she felt extremely tired as though she hadn't even been to bed. Well she hadn't and her back hurt.

"Hi, have you heard anything from Rosie or the hospital?" Lisa asked and tried her hardest to sound normal; she didn't want any awkward questions.

"No, no news is good news. Are you ready to go yet?" Margaret asked sharply.

Perhaps Margaret had had a bad night, too.

"I will be, give me an hour," Lisa replied.

"Okay I'll pick you up, at ten. Bye."

***

Margaret drove Lisa to collect her car, still parked in the street opposite the ruins of her friend's world. On stepping from Margaret's car, she had to hold onto the door. Lisa's knees felt weak, her legs went from under her. She felt sick as she looked at the fallen building which was once a quaint little coffee shop with history. So much had taken place there over the years and now nothing was left.

"Are you all right?" Margaret asked as she held Lisa's arm. She had quickly moved around the car to catch Lisa before she fell.

There Lisa stood just gazing at the pile of rubble.

"Oh, Margaret, what is Alison going to do?"

"Come on, it's only a building." Margaret was always to the point, but she was right; buildings could be rebuilt, but sometimes people couldn't. "Let's get to the hospital and pray we find Alison in a better condition. She is far more important than a pile of old bricks and wood."

Margaret was guiding Lisa to turn away. Yes, Lisa knew Alison was the important one, but nevertheless, there lay her life. The wooden frontage, some hundred years old, sprawled down the wooden steps now leading nowhere and the door was gone. Then she saw the little brass door bell had rolled down the footpath. Lisa let go of Margaret and walked over to pick it up. She would keep it for Alison.

"You okay to drive?" Margaret asked after looking down at the bell in Lisa's hand.

"Yes, I'll be fine. Will you follow me please?"

"Of course," Margaret said.

Both Lisa and Margaret pulled up into the car park of the hospital. And who were they to see but Danny stepping from a taxi? Margaret waved at him, knowing him better than Lisa. Danny's first wife had often dragged him into Margaret's craft shop, in the early days of its opening. She had also been a keen knitter, just like Margaret.

"Hello, you okay after your injuries Danny?" Margaret could see he had bandages on both hands and he limped a little on his left leg.

"Yes. I'll be fine. Have you come to see Alison?"

"Yes, we have and you?" Margaret asked.

"I have. I have always liked that lady." Margaret thought it was more than like and she smiled at him.

All three walked in together and went to reception to ask the whereabouts of Alison and if any visitors were allowed.

"No visitors," the receptionist replied.

Their faces dropped as they turned away.

"Let's go and see if Rosie is on duty," Lisa suggested.

They walked around the outside of the hospital and up to the doors of A and E. Should they go in and disturbed such a busy and important place?

"They must have a reception we can ask at, mustn't they?" Lisa said and led the way in.

Rosie wasn't in yet, as she had worked late the day before and no member of staff was allowed to tell them anything regarding Alison's health, as they weren't family. The receptionist could say she was in intensive care though. Nothing else could she divulge of any head wounds or the condition of her burns.

"We'll have to leave," Danny said.

Walking back across the car park, they bumped into Rosie.

"Hi, you're early for work; we were just told you wouldn't be in for some hours yet," Lisa explained in a rush.

"I came to sit with Alison for a while. I'm allowed in," and she pointed to her uniform, and smiled.

"What can you tell us?" Danny asked.

"I'm pretty confident she'll live, it's just in what condition, with that head injury and now I have said more than I should."

"Oh!" Both Lisa and Margaret said while Danny just looked on before speaking up again. "But we are her family; can't we visit?"

Margaret thought she could see Danny's eyes glisten.

"We'll come back tomorrow," Margaret said.

Rosie said she would try and get around the rules by explaining Alison had no family and that they were her best friends.

"Thank you, Rosie," Lisa said.

"Me too," Danny added.

"You too," and Rosie smiled at him even more. She was wondering if it was Alison and Danny on that love site.

Each of them left to go their separate ways, Rosie to the inside of a busy hospital and Danny was busy hailing a taxi.

Margaret had driven off home and Lisa turned to

ask if Danny would like a lift.

"That would be very kind of you," he said.

Lisa told him she wanted to go back and look at the coffee shop damage first. She didn't really know why, but she felt she had to.

"Okay." Danny didn't have a problem with that and remarked they may be able to find a few of Alison's treasured possessions, to rescue them for her and Lisa showed him the bell. He smiled.

Standing at the pile of rubble, it didn't appear that anything could be salvaged. The emergency vehicles and all their people had long since left and the gas vans that had been there were also missing, having made safe the area from any more gas leaks.

This visit wouldn't prove to be of any use to Alison.

"How are we likely to find anything more that's worth keeping from that mess?"

"I have her bell, Danny, let's leave it at that," Lisa said.

"I hear people are coming to pull down what's left of the old building tomorrow, to make safe the area from any more falling debris. Perhaps the demolition people will find the odd thing and put it aside for Alison," Danny said, placing his arm around Lisa's shoulder, in a gesture of kindness, nothing more.

"I think you're right," Lisa said.

"It's all taped off anyway. Look over there." He pointed to a huge sign with big red letters that spelled out DANGER.

Lisa and Danny were about to leave when

someone caught Lisa's eye. A man on the far side of the pile of rubble; he appeared to be watching them and he had seen Danny's arm around her.

"I'm off, you coming? I can walk home from here, it's not a problem," Danny told Lisa.

"I think I will stay a little longer, if you don't mind walking," Lisa said.

"Fine, see you soon, keep in touch," Danny said as he set off towards his apartment.

"I will," Lisa called after him feeling a little guilty as she watched him limp away.

Danny actually headed towards his place of work first which happened to only be two streets away. There were things he needed to check on. With his painful leg, he needed some time off work. He also wanted time to visit Alison.

Once Danny was out of sight she could turn to look to where she had seen that man standing, the man she thought she recognised.

He had disappeared.

"Oh damn it," she muttered. *It couldn't have been him, could it?*

Turning around to walk to her car she bumped right smack bang into Phil.

Chapter Eight
Phil

There he stood, close, in front of her, only inches away and twenty some odd years too.

"Phil!" she uttered, feeling flushed as she stepped away from him.

"Lisa," he said with a smile.

Lisa's heart flipped over at the sound of his voice. She hurt and grieved, her breathing stopped a second or two and restarted with a cough; she was going to die, right there in front of him. Her head was spinning, she felt sick. How could she feel all these things, all at the same time and after so long?

She fell into his arms for only a few seconds, then came to her senses and shouted at him.

"Get off, put me down."

"Lisa, I had to catch you. It really is you?"

"Well, you caught me, now let me go. And of course it's me; didn't you stop to think, I might have made a life here after you deserted me?"

Phil stood back now and just looked at this woman before him. He knew she was no longer the young school girl he courted, who turned into a young mum, who he had left so long ago. A love he should never have left behind. Here stood a good looking confident woman before him.

"Well, we can't stand here all day, looking at each other." Phil spoke first, as Lisa was in no fit state to say any more, as much as she wanted to.

She was still trying to breath in some sort of rhythm after blurting out her last sentence.

"I would say, come for a coffee, but..." and he waved his arm towards the coffee shop which was no more.

"Coffee! With you? No thanks." Lisa had found her voice again. She turned to walk to her car, but he grabbed her arm to stop her leaving.

"Let go," she shouted. "How dare you?"

"I'm so sorry. But I have to talk to you," Phil said.

"Why don't you just go to Alison's bedside? After all it was her you were going to meet." Lisa couldn't help herself.

"You know about that?" Phil looked surprised.

"Of course, I know about that. I'm her friend. Were you going to enjoy her and then walk away?"

That's not fair, he thought; but she did have a point. There had been many women over the years and in many ports around the world too but none were ever like his Lisa.

"I'm going now," she said and brushed him aside.

She knew she shouldn't have been so rude as to say that and she ran to her car, jumped in and went speeding off. She slowed when she turned into the next road. She realised she was doing too much of this speeding lark these days and would inevitably get caught and she didn't want a ticket.

Phil couldn't return to his car in time to follow her. He stood and watched her go, unsure of what to do next.

He would have to think of some other way to find

out where she lived and he wondered if his baby girl, Beth, still lived with her mother. Baby, he thought. No, she is no longer a baby. He knew she would be twenty five because he always sent money to her bank account on the date of her birthday.

Perhaps she is married herself with children of her own. He could be a grandfather. Phil quietly smiled to himself. He rather liked the idea of being a granddad.

Chapter Nine
Help

Lisa collapsed in her chair at home, Barney at her feet. What was she going to do? Who could she talk to? Not Margaret, she would just tell her to get rid of Phil. She wouldn't understand the turmoil she was in.

After all, Phil was Beth's father, her children's grandfather. Did she have the right to know where Phil was and not tell their daughter? But she didn't know where he was, did she? Tears of anger filled Lisa's eyes as she ran her fingers through her brown, bobbed hair.

Barney barked. He heard someone walking up their path. No it couldn't be, Lisa thought; had Phil followed her?

Slowly she walked along her hall, stopped to check her face and hair in the mirror; she shook her head with a question, do I care? She went to turn the door handle and then thought to shout and ask who was there.

"It's me, Rosie."

"Rosie." Lisa relaxed and opened the door. "Am I glad to see you; come on in."

"Whatever's the matter? You look like you've seen a ghost," Rosie said.

"I have; he's part of my past. Come in," and she pointed Rosie to her sitting room. "Would you like a drink?" Lisa meant something stronger than tea or coffee. Rosie understood and asked if she had any white wine in the place.

Lisa said she thought she had, even though she wasn't a great drinker herself. She went to the cupboard in her sitting room and there she found a bottle of Sauvignon, left over from Christmas.

"Will this do?" Lisa held the bottle up to show Rosie.

"Yap, fine, let's drink and you tell me all."

"Well, okay; I've got to tell someone or I'll go crazy," said Lisa. "But you must promise me you will keep it to yourself. I mean that, Rosie. You mustn't tell anyone, under any circumstances, especially not anyone at the hospital. It must remain between the two of us. Do you swear?"

Rosie nodded, realising the seriousness of the situation.

Beth had trained and become a nurse at that hospital, and although she was on maternity leave at the moment, what Lisa was about to tell Rosie, would soon get back to her.

Rosie poured two glasses, full, almost to their brims, with white wine. She had a feeling they were going to need it all and damn to the headache that might follow; would follow.

Sitting upright in her chair, grasping her hands tight around her wine glass so as not to spill any, Lisa began her story.

Rosie was more relaxed and had her feet curled up on Lisa's sofa, wine glass in hand. She listened with intent, sipping all the time at her wine.

"Okay, so that's all very interesting but it happened years back, what's that got to do with today? Or why you look so dreadful?"

Lisa had filled Rosie in, on all her years from school and meeting Phil, getting married and moving to this place, to having Beth and Phil leaving.

Rosie poured herself another glass of wine. She lifted the bottle in Lisa's direction; Lisa shook her head. She had hardly touched the first glass and she carried on talking.

"Well, he's back."

"What? Phil." Rosie coughed over her mouthful of wine. "Never!"

"Yes, Phil." Lisa sounded agitated now and carried on. "He was standing in front of the rubble that was once the coffee shop."

"No?" Rosie was astounded. "What, I mean, did he say anything?"

Lisa spoke of their exchange of words and that she drove off, leaving him standing on the spot, looking lost, rather like she had left him standing in the school playground once, when they fell out over her parents.

"So why was he there, at the coffee shop? You haven't said, did he say?" Rosie was intrigued and wondered how she was going to keep all this juicy information to herself. But she knew she must.

Lisa now wondered if she should say anymore, because that would involve Alison who wouldn't want the world knowing her business.

"No," Lisa said rather sheepishly.

Rosie thought there was more to this part of the story than Lisa was letting on.

Lisa suddenly realised she hadn't asked Rosie

why she had called round in the first place and asked that very question.

"Oh, yes, I came to tell you. Alison will be fine. She has come round and is sitting up. She has a terrible headache and a burns bandage on one arm which she has in a sling for the moment. Plus of course there are many bruises just beginning to come out all over her body; she took quite a battering, you know. It won't be long before she is black and blue. The doctors are going to keep her in for a few days under observation and to carry out another head scan and replace the bandages on her burns."

"Can she have visitors?" Lisa asked.

"No visitors allowed for the time being. She needs complete rest. Given time she should be as good as new. Of course she will have to return to have the bandages replaced every so often and another scan on her head before she is allowed to leave hospital."

Lisa knew rest was what she would need as well as understanding with the shock of losing everything, her home, its contents and her business.

"When she leaves hospital, where will she go to live?" Lisa asked.

"I hadn't thought of that," Rosie said.

"She will have to come here. I have Beth's old room free, now she's left home."

"That's very kind of you. Can I tell Alison that?"

"Why yes, of course." Lisa smiled.

"Well I must be off," Rosie said as she stood to leave. "Thanks for the wine. Glad I'm not driving."

Rosie almost got to the door and turned, "I almost

forgot. A man named Danny who was also treated for minor injuries tried to visit; do you know him?"

"Yes, he's the bread delivery man; he arrives early every morning at the coffee shop." Lisa explained he must have been there when it happen.

"There was another man too, but he didn't leave a name," Rosie said. "Right I'm really off now, bye."

"Bye, Rosie thanks for coming."

What Lisa wanted to say was, 'keep your mouth shut' but she wouldn't be so rude and said instead: "don't forget, what I have told you doesn't leave my house."

"Yes, that's fine, but I really don't know how to advise you." Rosie walked off down the path to catch a bus.

Lisa took a guess at who the other man might be. Phil.

Chapter Ten
A Friend to Stay

The time had come for Alison to leave the hospital. It was a sunny afternoon and only a short time since Alison and Lisa's lives had been turned upside down.

Lisa had popped in a couple of evenings, in that second week, to visit and as far as she knew Phil hadn't been near again. Margaret reminded Lisa that the hospital had said *no visitors,* but that had been when Alison lay unconscious; she would wait until Alison went home. Lisa thought this a silly thing for Margaret to say; had she forgotten, Alison had no home to go to?

Lisa felt Margaret had used that no visitors rule as an excuse not to go in, when she knew full well it was at Alison's request after she was able to talk, that she had no visitors because she looked dreadful with all her bruises and swollen face.

Lisa heard later, via Rosie, that the unknown man had tried to visit again one afternoon and had been turned away.

Pulling into the car park, Lisa didn't see Phil sitting in a year old, very clean silver Mercedes parked in the lane, two rows in front of her. She had been distracted by Danny coming up to her car window, which she had rolled down so she could talk with him.

"Hi, come to see Alison?" Danny was asking Lisa

as she turned her loud music off.

"Actually, I'm picking her up to take her home to mine."

"That's good of you," Danny said.

"Just until she is fully recovered and able to find a place of her own," Lisa explained.

"Okay if I come in with you?" Danny was hoping to be involved in Alison's recovery.

"Yes, of course. Why don't you come back with us and have a cup of tea?" Lisa invited Danny, thinking Alison might like that.

She knew Margaret would think it a good idea, after her matchmaking once before and perhaps she could steer Alison away from Phil, not for herself but for Alison's sake.

"Thanks. That would be great," Danny said.

He was pleased; he cared for Alison and wanted to be close. He had asked her out before, only on those occasions it hadn't come across as a date but to be his plus one at functions, all to do with his business and likewise she had taken him to her coffee business meetings.

Margaret had commented on Danny's affections for Alison when the three friends were having coffee that morning, only a few days before the explosion.

Phil watched as Lisa and Danny walked towards the hospital together. He was trying to work out who Danny was and the connection with his wife. It was true they had never divorced and he was glad.

She had never asked or wanted anything from him. The money he had placed in Beth's bank account as a standing order on each of her birthdays and every Christmas had been his doing; she had never asked for anything, in fact didn't even know where he lived. This money had grown into a tidy amount over the years but neither woman had touched it. Both had agreed when Beth turned eighteen, that she would keep it safely in the bank for her wedding. Lisa and Beth both knew they would never find that sort of money for a wedding, and why shouldn't Beth have her father pay for it, even if he wasn't going to be there? Lisa had tried to hold bad thoughts about him, to try and make his leaving easier but they never lasted for long.

Beth still dreamed of the day when she would meet her dad. Although she had not forgiven him for what he had done to her mother, he was still her father and she wanted to know him, perhaps have him walk her up the aisle, one day. To have her father give her away was her dream. Lisa had never fully explained why he left, she only reassured Beth he loved her and it wasn't her fault in any way.

Once, Lisa and Beth had asked the bank for his details, to try and trace him, but of course the bank wouldn't give out that information. '*The Data protection Act.*' She knew that now but had been young then and Lisa hadn't pushed to find him since. Now Beth was a mother and hadn't the time or the inclination to try to find her father. And still the money grew.

Phil sat in his car and patiently waited for whoever would come from that hospital. His plan was to follow Lisa, hopefully to her home, to see where she lived. What next he wasn't sure but he was feeling a little guilty for using Alison to find out about Lisa and Beth.

A couple of hours later, Alison came walking out of the hospital with Lisa and Danny either side of her. Danny helped Alison get into the back of Lisa's car.

"Would you like me to drive so you can sit with Alison?" Danny asked.

"Are you insured to drive my car?"

"Yes, goes with my job," Danny replied.

"Well, yes then, if your leg is okay."

"It is; you have an automatic, don't you?"

Lisa moved to the back alongside Alison.

This confused Phil who was trying to work out which woman this man was with.

He had watched Lisa drive in and then this man had appeared as if from nowhere to walk with her and now he was driving two women somewhere. Which woman was he with? It must be Alison; after all she was the one online looking for love. Maybe Alison did this thing of having two or even more men taking her out.

No, just because that's something he had thought of doing in the past, he didn't think so, which meant Danny was with Lisa. He smiled to himself and almost gloated because he knew they couldn't marry and now he wanted another chance to win Lisa back. He had suddenly had a jolt of jealousy. He wondered wherever that had come from because, like Lisa, he had also tried to bury his feelings and get on with life.

He started his car to follow the group now in Lisa's car. It wasn't long before Danny pulled up outside Lisa's house. Phil parked further back down the street and looked at the house in surprise. She still lived in the same house as he had lived with her.

He watched them walk up the path, go in through the door. Danny bent down to rub at a black dog. Phil was surprised again; they have a dog. Oh, happy families; he couldn't watch anymore and after Danny shut the door behind him and the two women, Phil took off.

He hadn't expected to feel like this, he hadn't thought about how he might feel after twenty odd years.

His Lisa had what he had never found, from the day he had left them, a dog, a family, happiness and all because that man must be her partner. Phil drove, not sure where he was going or what he was going to do next.

Indoors, Alison was settling herself on the sofa while Lisa made tea and Danny sat in the chair opposite Alison just looking at her with eyes like Barney's, a soppy old dog.

"Why are you so quiet and looking at me like that," she asked.

Danny just grinned but didn't have a chance to answer as Lisa carried a tray of mugs full of tea and a plate of ginger bread cake into the room.

"Lovely, just what we needed." Now Danny spoke.

Lisa asked Alison how she was doing and if there was anything she wanted. At those words Alison burst into tears. Danny leaped from his chair, to sit close by her and placed his arm around her shoulders.

"I'm so sorry," Lisa said.

Through her sobs, Alison tried to explain. It was all too much; her release from the hospital and Lisa being so kind to invite her to stay and what Danny had tried to do that day of the explosion.

"I did nothing," he said and he looked rather embarrassed.

Lisa looked at Danny with enquiring eyes. What had he done and why was he there at that time in the morning?

Alison couldn't talk and took a sip of tea.

Danny took her hands as she placed her mug down on the tray on the coffee table. He held them gently while Lisa looked on in surprise. She could now see what Margaret had been saying, Danny did care for Alison. No it was far more than that; he was in love with her and Alison couldn't see it.

"Danny, tell me, why were you at the coffee shop when it all happened?" Lisa hoped she might gain some information. She had heard on that dreadful day one of the firemen say that if it hadn't been for Danny, Alison would have been killed.

"Oh it was just my usual deliveries."

"On a Sunday?"

Danny wouldn't expand on that.

Alison had stopped sobbing and removed her hands from Danny's. She sat upright after slouching, apologised and felt she was in control once more.

"Sorry about what?" Lisa asked. "You don't have to be apologising to me."

She looked across at Danny.

"Nor me," he added. "No, come on, we're going to help you get back on your feet, find you somewhere to live and work."

"That's if you want to work, of course," Lisa added.

Danny felt perhaps they were pushing her too quickly.

"First of all, we must go shopping and buy you some new clothes, when you feel up to it, of course," Lisa felt she was telling her what she needed to do and said, "or we could just look online and choose some outfits. Get them delivered; that could be fun."

Lisa was trying to cheer Alison up, but she had inadvertently mentioned, online.

"The man I was going to meet," Alison touched her cheek, "he might have been at the shop. Did anyone see him?"Alison blurted out.

Danny looked disappointed when hearing her concerns for a man he didn't know about, while Lisa stood to remove mugs and tray back to the kitchen, hence avoiding this conversation.

"There were many onlookers there that day," Danny said and followed Lisa into the kitchen. "What's she talking about? What man?" he asked.

Lisa shrugged before speaking.

"Oh, just someone we three girls had seen on a dating site. We were having a bit of fun one day that was all."

Danny wasn't stupid and didn't buy into that as a reason.

"Was he dating Alison?" Danny was feeling extremely disappointed now. He had been working up to asking Alison out on a proper date.

"No, it was just a bit of fun, I tell you. Alison

hasn't got a boyfriend."

Lisa moved passed him and went back to sit with Alison.

"Perhaps you should go for a lie down," Lisa suggested. "The hospital said you could only come home with me if I took care of you and made sure you rested."

"I'll be off then," Danny said and left but not before he bent over and kissed Alison on her forehead.

His kiss made Alison smile and she remember he had been her hero. He had saved her life and no one else knew why he had been at her place.

Chapter Eleven
Consequence of Men

After Lisa had made sure Alison was happy with the spare room which had once been Beth's and still the walls held the pictures from her teenage days, Lisa went down to phone her daughter. By now her grandchildren should be settled, one in a bed and the other in his Moses basket set by Beth's side; he would soon want his next feed.

Babies could be very demanding; she remembered her only one and felt sad she never had the chance for another. After Phil left there had never been another man in her life. That had been her choice.

Then after all this time there he stood, as large as life in front of her and all she could do was collapse, albeit for only a second or so, but how embarrassing and to think she still felt something inside for him.

As she sat in her kitchen her thoughts wandered back over so many years before the phone rang. An hour had passed as she finished off the white wine left from the other evening with Rosie and the ringing made her jump half out of her skin. She took a quick glance at the clock; oh damn, I was going to phone her. Lisa picked up the receiver.

"Hello, I was going to phone you," Lisa had seen Beth's name on the display.

"Hi, mum, did you get Alison home okay?"

"Yes, she's resting in your old room. How's

baby, got a name yet?" she said flippantly.

"No mum," and Lisa heard Beth sigh at the other end of the line.

She thought better of it, than to mention a wedding, which she had been thinking of earlier that day and the paying for it, with Phil's little nest egg, well, Beth's nest egg.

Mother and daughter chatted for a while, before a tiny baby cried for his supper.

"Can't Andy see to the baby?" Lisa asked.

"Well, he's not in yet," Beth quickly said.

Lisa decided to leave it; she didn't want to upset Beth.

"Have to go mum, talk soon, love you," and she cut off.

Lisa went about her tidying before bedtime routine, trying her best to be quiet, thinking Alison would be asleep.

She was trying not to think badly of Andy still being out when, as she saw it, her daughter needed him at her side.

Far from being asleep, Alison had lain quietly on the bed, going over and over what had happened to her in the past couple of weeks and what might happen in her near future. Already she was thinking she couldn't impose on Lisa for too long. She knew she was insured on the coffee shop building and contents but it wouldn't take long to lose her trade to other outlets in the middle of town, some of which might be found to be more convenient to a few of her customers.

That thought took her mind to suppliers and

deliveries. Danny. What could she make of Danny? She wasn't sure and had him jumping around in her mind. That thought made her sit up in her bed. Did he fancy her? No, surely not but a doubt had crept in. Did she fancy him? Alison had never looked at him in that way before and she wasn't sure what to think.

She patted her pillows, straightened her duvet and flopped back to wonder. Danny had been around her for years. She remembered his wife, such a nice lady. She died without giving him children. That was sad and she remembered how she had wanted children herself, but after so long had brushed that thought from her mind and built a successful coffee shop business instead.

She had moved with the times and now sold all manner of coffee flavours presented in a mix of vessels. Anything her customers wanted, she tried to give them.

As her thoughts turned from coffees to cakes and doughnuts, sandwiches, French crispy bread, her mind returned to Danny and his deliveries. What was it about Danny she liked?

She tried to dismiss him from her thoughts and think about the stranger, the photo of the handsome man online, Phil, the man she hadn't met. Had he turned up that day of the explosion? Did he get caught up in it? Was he safe? So many questions, she would have to ask Lisa in the morning, if she knew. The biggest question in Alison's head was should she pursue this Phil person and her adventure of *looking for love* on the internet? With that thought lingering, she fell asleep.

***

"Morning, did you sleep well?" Lisa asked Alison as she walked slowly into Lisa's kitchen.

"Yes thanks, I did, after a lot of thinking."

Lisa wasn't going to ask her what she had been thinking. She could guess much of it and didn't want to hear it, or discuss it.

"Anything to eat?" Lisa asked as she opened her fridge and cupboards to show her normal choice of breakfast.

"Toast and a cup of tea will be great," Alison replied and sat herself down at Lisa's breakfast bar.

Bending over to make a fuss of Barney made Alison hold her head; it still hurt her.

"You okay?" Lisa asked holding out a hand for her to grab.

"It's nothing. I'll be fine."

Both women ate their toast and marmalade and said little. Neither was used to having company at the breakfast table.

"Shall we do a bit of shopping online this morning? You could really do with your own clothes."

"Yes," Alison said. "I have nothing," and a tear trickled down her face.

"I'm sorry, I didn't mean to upset you," and Lisa moved to place an arm around Alison's shoulders.

"I'm just being silly. Let's do it. It was kind of you to lend me some of your clothes but I do need my own."

The two women settled themselves close on the sofa and started searching the internet. One would say how about this, the other would turn their nose up or perhaps say, 'it's okay.' This went on for a while and once they had a basket full of clothes and accessories, Alison suggested maybe she should cut it down a bit. She went through the tops, trousers and dresses, as well as the nightwear and underwear again. When she got to those last two items Alison wondered what type of thing she should wear on a date with the man on the internet.

But then Danny's face popped back into her mind, what would he like?

No, Danny is not interested in me or me in him; she felt cross with herself and brushed the thought aside for a second time in twenty four hours.

"Alison, you're blushing, are you feeling ill?" Lisa asked.

Alison just smiled

Actually it was what she was thinking, not how she was feeling; underwear, nightwear, men.

That first week at Lisa's, Alison tried not to give the man on the internet anymore thoughts but Danny did keep popping around in person for an hour or two, to check on her.

The clothes arrived over the next couple of days and Alison had great fun trying them on and giving Lisa a fashion show in her sitting room. Both women, by the end of that first week, found they had enjoyed themselves immensely.

Beth called to spend a day, bringing her children and Alison found after lunch she needed a rest and went to her bed.

"Is she doing okay?" Beth asked her mother.

"Yes, she just gets tired and worries about her future."

Six o'clock arrived. Beth had fed baby and Alison was up again. It was time for Beth to go.

"I'm off mum," Beth said and kissed Lisa on the cheek.

Lily pulled at her grandmother to pick her up. Lisa held baby in her arms and passed him to Beth. She picked Lily up, planted kisses all over her face and neck and hugged her granddaughter. The little girl giggled and Alison looked on. How she would have loved to be in Lisa's position.

Lisa had refrained from asking about babies' names, or Andy and his work and even weddings on this visit. Actually she didn't always mention these subjects, it was a standing joke that was wearing thin with Beth.

Her house was quiet once again and Lisa tidied around before making dinner.

"Here let me help." Alison stood up but Lisa told her to sit and rest.

"Why don't you use my laptop and have a play around on the games," Lisa suggested.

Alison told her she wouldn't know where to start with games and Lisa opened with her password the different sites, so that Alison could go wherever she wanted on her machine.

While Lisa was busy in the kitchen, Alison found herself on the love site. She logged in and the red hearts began falling across the screen again before her name popped up and suddenly there was Phil. Why it surprised her, she wasn't sure. He had written a good few times since she was last online. He was asking when she had access to e-mail to write back to him.

Alison felt awkward and took a quick look around in case Lisa came back into the room. Why she felt this guilt she really didn't know, but she worried, after all Lisa had helped her find the site and set it up, so she could follow it, so why feel like this? She instinctively shrugged and then her fingers struck the keys.

Phil, she wrote, I'm so glad you are well and didn't get caught up in the explosion. You are all right, aren't you?

Alison automatically closed the laptop lid as Lisa suddenly reappeared and leaned over the back of the sofa and touched her shoulders.

"I know it's a Tuesday evening, but I cooked a chicken roast, that okay with you?"

"Yes, lovely, it smells delicious."

"What are you hiding then?" Lisa laughed: "only joking, you don't have to say."

"No that's fine, you can look, don't know why I did that, force of habit I suppose, what with the running of a business. Here take a look."

There was Phil's face looking right back at Lisa. She straightened up and turned quickly back to her kitchen.

Alison thought it a bit odd but then again, Lisa had food boiling on the hob and roasting in the oven. She thought no more of it, while Lisa was taking deep breaths, leaning against the kitchen worktop to steady herself from her spinning head.

"Pull yourself together woman," she muttered under her breath.

The dinner went well and no more was mentioned about men that night.

Chapter Twelve
Time Goes By

The weeks went quickly by. The two women got on well, considering they had each been used to living on their own for a number of years. Hospital visits came and went for Alison and then, on one of the last visits, Phil sat in the car park.

Alison had forgotten she told him when chatting online that she was going for her burns check up. She had gone on her own on this occasion as Lisa was babysitting for Beth.

Phil jumped from his car and startled Alison.

"Hello there," he said.

"Oh hello, what are you doing here?"

"I wondered if I could escort you."

"Escort me?" Alison said.

"You know what I mean, can I come in with you and perhaps after your appointment we could stop and have a coffee in the concourse they have at this hospital."

Alison had a slight grin on her face when she turned away from him and said, "Okay if you like."

Phil locked his car. He didn't really know where this meeting was taking him or why he was really here. It just seemed a good idea at the time.

Walking into the outpatients department, Alison felt self-conscious about this man she had only just met in the flesh, and knew very little of, walking next to her. Panic hit her when she saw Beth walking towards her and then stopped to speak.

"Hi Alison, how are you doing?"

Alison introduced Phil as a friend and Beth as her friend's daughter.

"Pleased to meet you," Beth said with a lovely smile which showed off the one dimple in her cheek. She held out her hand to shake his and he held it longer than he perhaps should have.

"Sorry," he said and removed his hand after studying her face.

Beth just smiled at him.

Alison asked if she was well and then realised she had introduced these two people without giving their names.

"Yes, just here for a check up after having the baby."

There had been a few problems at the birth, but Beth wasn't going into that.

Phil had walked off when the baby word was mentioned. Women's talk was coming he thought and was polite enough to move away.

"I must be off; mum is babysitting." Beth turned to take another look at Phil, who waved back at her.

"Bye, nice to have met you," Beth called to Phil and he nodded.

Did she know him? It bothered Beth all the way home. That handshake had lingered far too long.

"She seemed a pleasant woman," Phil said to Alison as he returned to her side. "She looked familiar somehow. What was her name?"

"Oh sorry, I meant to say, that was Beth, she's Lisa girl."

Phil stopped in his tracks, and took a breath. Alison had to stop and turn to see where he had got to. She called to him.

"Phil, you coming with me?" she asked.

"Yes, fine," and he had to pull himself together very quickly so that Alison didn't ask any awkward questions.

Alison's appointment went well and she was finally discharged by her consultant.

"Let's go for that coffee now," Phil said.

He needed it, black and strong ideally with an alcohol shot in it. He knew that wouldn't happen here.

"Yes, let's," and Alison headed towards the queue.

Alison felt so much more relaxed than she had in weeks, only Phil didn't.

She was finished with all her hospital visits and could concentrate on rebuilding her life. She wondered if this man, now sitting himself down at a small round table with his coffee in hand and smiling at her, would have a place in her future life.

"You are looking well," Phil said to her, trying to act normally.

"I feel it."

He then went on to ask about her plans for the future and if she would open another coffee shop. Now having met Beth he had no idea what his future held.

The coffee shop subject had been eating away at Alison for some time, but it always made her feel sad and reminded her of what she had lost. Not only her income, but the people she saw every week, everyday.

The history in the old place, the eighteenth century ghost she thought she saw hovering at the top of the stairs on occasion. She remembered the people who had declared their love for each other in her crowded place five years earlier, brought about through a once in a lifetime rain storm.

A tear reached her eye and gently trickled down her cheek.

"I'm so very sorry. I didn't mean to upset you," Phil said.

"It's silly; I'm just still a bit emotional," Alison was saying to Phil when suddenly a man placed his hands down on their table with a thud. Leaning forward his face was pushed almost into Phil's face.

"You upsetting my lady?" Danny shouted at Phil, having seen her wipe away that tear.

"No, Danny, of course he's not," Alison said as she raised her eyes to glare at him.

Danny stood back from Phil but still looked hard at him, before Alison asked him to join them for coffee. Alison firmly invited Danny to sit down, pulling out a chair to her other side. She did the introductions with names this time and both men shook hands across the table. Each sat either side of Alison now and still they eyed each other, as though Alison was the prize.

A quick thought flashed through Phil's mind; this man had called Alison his lady, where did that leave Lisa?

***

"Hi mum, I'm home. Kids been all right while I've been gone?"

Lisa told her they had been *as good as gold*, but then all grandmas would say that, Beth thought and smiled to herself.

"Baby is asleep and had his feed. How did you get on?"

"Yes, everything back in order," Beth reassure her mother. Then she added: "you won't believe who I saw Alison with, in the hospital."

"No who?"

"A man!"

"Never, who was he?"

"I don't know, but he was rather handsome for an older man."

"Beth, behave." Her mum laughed. "Well did he have a name?"

"Well, it was very odd. Alison didn't give a name but as they walked away I heard her call him Phil."

Lisa had to sit down.

"Mum, you okay? You've gone quite pale, what's the matter?"

"Nothing, I come over like this every now and then, it's my age. Funny old bodies we women have; the men would never cope."

"That's for sure," Beth said, having just given birth. "One baby would be their lot," and both women laughed as Andy came in, smiling all over his face.

"You're early," Beth said as they kissed each other.

"What's so funny?" He asked.

"Nothing," Beth said. The two women just smiled at each other.

Andy was grinning from ear to ear when he picked up Lily and swung her around in his arms, telling her she was his sweetie before placing her back on the floor where her little legs wobbled from her dizziness.

Beth told him he looked as though he was the cat that got the cream.

"Well, yes of course, what more could I wish for. I have you," and he put his arm around Beth; "and now two beautiful children."

Lisa butted in "and a very helpful mother-in-law, who baby-sits."

"Mum, stop it." Lisa knew they weren't married.

"Oh yes. I forgot. So what's my title then?"

Andy just laughed and winked at her.

"So why are you home early?" Beth asked him.

"I'm starting two weeks holiday with a bonus."

"Wow, really? That's great," and Beth turned to Lily: "Daddy's going to be home with us," and Lily started jumping up and down, shouting, "Daddy, Daddy play with me."

"I will, honey, I just have to tell Mummy something."

Beth was eagerly waiting.

"Come on then, what is it?"

"I have my promotion, which comes with loads more money to spoil you with."

Lily didn't understand what daddy meant but she knew the word spoil and hung onto his legs, giggling.

Beth understood and hugged Andy so hard he could hardly breathe.

"Well done," she said and kissed him again.

Lisa left after congratulating Andy and was happy on her drive home. She played her music extra loud and was singing along with it, just as she and Phil had years ago.

All her reservations were over. Why couldn't she have trusted Andy in the first place, instead of worrying where he was every evening?

Unfortunately the treatment she had encountered in her life had made her think the worst of people, often not giving them the benefit of the doubt.

She remembered what her old great grandmother had told her once, when she was a little girl.

People will make you distrust, when you have been hurt. People can make you what you are, so remember dear, be yourself. Not all people are bad; sometimes things are done with the best of intentions.

And so Andy had been out in the evening working for his family and Phil had never forgotten his daughter and sent that money. Lisa was forgiving and she felt good. Thanks great granny.

Lisa was still smiling when she reached her front door and turned her key. Happy days, if only Beth and Andy were married, her life would feel perfect and she sighed as she walked in, stopped to kick her shoes off and thought, after all it was their life, not hers and she must stop thinking about a marriage; only baby must be given a name soon, bless him.

These two things would make Lisa ecstatic, or so she thought and she pondered over these thoughts when a black dog came running up to her.

"Hello there, Barney. Did you miss me? Is Alison home yet?"

"Yes I'm in the kitchen," Alison called out.

"How did you get on at the hospital?"

"Fine, all signed off. I saw your Beth there." Alison didn't mention Danny or Phil.

"Yes, Beth said."

Lisa was having the perfect day; all was well with her daughter's household and here now with Alison.

"Let's get some dinner and perhaps talk about where you go from here, Alison."

"Why, you fed up with me living here?" Alison kept a straight face as she said this but for only a few seconds before laughing.

Lisa laughed too.

Chapter Thirteen
Phil or Danny

The following morning Alison told Lisa she was off out. That was after the postman had delivered the letter she now held in her hand, the letter she had been waiting for. The offer from the insurance company had at long last arrived, and it was enough to rebuild her coffee shop. She had also been advised to sue the gas company; she would see about that later.

"I'm off to see an architect, the one the estate agent put me in touch with."

"Okay, good luck," Lisa said as Alison left the house.

Suddenly it was quiet and Lisa looked around, wondering what she was going to do with herself today. She had no idea. She had been working as a temp in different offices before all this happened with Alison and Beth's new baby. She had cut her work right back while both women needed her, but she didn't mind. The joy of life for her was helping people and her babies were just the best. But now she must pick up some work again; she needed the money. Beth was coping and Alison would soon be moving out, leaving her to make her own life. She was about to lift her phone, to contact the agency for some temp work when it rang; it was Danny, asking after Alison. Lisa explained she was out and about in town shopping. She left it open, as to what Alison was actually doing. That was Alison's business and not for her to say.

Lisa made her call, they could offer her a few hours work.

"Now what shall we do, Barney, how about we go for a walk in the park?"

Barney understood the word *walk* and dashed off to where his lead hung on a hook near the back door.

Reaching the park, Lisa sat with Barney by her side. The sun was warm and she watched the little ones with their parents. Swings floated back and forth, see-saws went up and down and the roundabout made Lisa's eyes dizzy. A few happy children squealed now and then.

She had never told Beth how she wished she had had more children and again she was quietly pleased Beth had two. Not that it was any of her business; she knew that and now kept out of Beth's and Andy's decisions. How very different to only a few years back when she had interfered and now she regretted it. After all she had worked hard not to be like her parents.

Lisa smiled and ruffled Barneys head.

"It all turned out okay, didn't it boy?" she said and the dog barked as though he understood. Or perhaps it was because someone came up from behind her bench.

"What turned out okay?" It was Phil asking. "May I sit?"

"It's a free country," Lisa said.

Why didn't she say no? It was too late; he was sitting on the same bench as her with his hands clasped tightly between his knees. He had left a large gap between them and she made sure she used both hands to hold Barney's lead.

"You come here often?" He asked with a silly smirk on his face, his one dimple showing.

"Shut up," Lisa said and pulled on Barney's collar, when he tried to stand to walk off. "Sit boy," she said.

"I am, sitting," Phil said and winked at her.

"Oh, you're infuriating, you always were."

"But you loved me."

Lisa stood to walk off.

"Don't go." Phil grabbed her arm to pull her back.

"I've told you before, don't do that."

"Sorry." And he let go and patted the bench.

Lisa sat down and quietly waited for him to say something; then they both spoke together.

"Sorry," they said, together.

"This is ridiculous," Lisa moaned. "I'm going home."

"We need to talk," Phil said seriously now.

"It's a bit late for that, isn't it? How many years has it been?" And Phil said the exact amount, to the very day.

Lisa was taken aback. She knew how many but never dreamed he would remember.

"Talk about what?" Lisa asked, "Our daughter?"

"A divorce," he said.

She wasn't expecting that and her mouth dropped open.

"Well, I guessed that's what you would want

after all this time," he said. "I'm surprised you haven't been in touch before to ask for one, especially as you have been living with that man."

"What man?"

"The one I saw you with the other day."

Lisa stood; she suddenly felt the stinging of tears forming at the backs of her eyes. She was furious, really angry at him, but there was no way she would let him see this and she certainly wasn't going to explain Danny to him.

"Put it in writing!" she screamed and marched off.

He pretended he didn't know her address and called after her for it.

"Same place. Never moved," she shouted back at him and still she walked.

She couldn't turn and show her tear stained face to him. She had her pride after all. She began to walk quicker and quicker until she was running with Barney alongside.

People stared as she passed them, one woman even turned and asked if she was okay, but Lisa just ran on and out of the park.

When they reached her front door she landed up sitting on the step, after dropping her keys. Barney was still panting for all his worth when Alison arrived shortly afterwards.

"What have you two been up to? Just look at the state of the pair of you. Come on in. I'll make tea for us."

Alison wouldn't ask what was wrong, she would wait for Lisa to explain, if she wanted to. Lisa didn't want to; she couldn't. She had been sitting that afternoon with the man pictured on the internet, when it should have been Alison spending time with him.

Lisa couldn't talk to her daughter and Rosie hadn't been around to see her again, not even a phone call. Some friend she was, Lisa thought but then they weren't close friends. She didn't have a very close friend really, just lots of people she knew, chatted to and had coffee with, like Alison and Margaret. Phil had been her best friend at school and during her early life and yet more tears rolled down her cheeks.

Lisa had had to be independent all her life. Her mother hadn't wanted her and her father was too busy being a bully to her or working with the needy people within his church. Then she was left on her own, with baby Beth. She had kept herself mostly to herself while bringing up her child alone. Oh how her head hurt from all these thoughts.

Margaret came to mind; Lisa was now wondering where she had been all these weeks. Keeping out of her way, in case there might be work to do, not wanting to get involved.

"That was about right," she said aloud.

"What was that?" Alison asked.

"Did you give Barney water to drink?" Lisa pretended that was what she had said. Then realised she was being too hard on Margaret.

After the tea was drunk in silence, Lisa felt she ought to ask how the meeting went that morning with the architect.

"Yeah, fine, good. He's going to start on some drawings which he thinks will get passed easily enough by the council. He'll phone when his outline sketches are ready."

Alison was holding back until she felt Lisa was in a better mood. She didn't want to show too much excitement when she knew Lisa had been crying.

Lisa smiled and showed some interest.

"You won't believe who the architect is?" Alison didn't wait for Lisa to ask. "It's only Phil off the internet."

Alison had thought it strange that he hadn't mentioned his work when they had coffee in the hospital.

"No!"

And Lisa ran from the sitting room to her bedroom and slammed the door behind her. She didn't know if she was going to be sick in her en-suite or just collapse onto her bed. She did neither. She went to the top of her wardrobe and pulled down a pretty pink flowered box while swearing words she didn't even know she knew, when the box flew out of her hands and spilled its contents all over the floor.

Why didn't he say he had seen Alison when they sat in the park? Her head was in a whirl with all her thoughts. Why the secret, Phil?

Sitting on her very old sheepskin rug, the one they brought back from Wales so long ago, she started sifting through the photos and other bits and pieces of sentimental value that she kept stored away.

She also thought she had stored Phil, her first love, her only love away. As her memories lay all around her, her love for Phil bubbled up to the surface and it hurt, oh, how it hurt.

There lay the photo of the bed and breakfast house tucked away in a narrow lane just up from a remote beach. That had been their first long weekend away together. There had been few people about and often they had that beach all to themselves. The weather was warm as was their love for each other and soon she would be taken by surprise when her feeling turned into a burning for him.

Lisa had told her parents she was staying with an old school friend; how she had got away with that still amazed her. It was on that beach that Beth was conceived. Lisa was so naive; she hadn't thought she would fall pregnant on her first time.

Both had been nervous but Phil had taken her to a pretty spot amongst the sand dunes where the gulls flew above, out across a deep grey sea that gently rolled in leaving a sound that washed her mind away. He took her slowly to another place; he was kind and caring to her needs. He told her how much he loved her and how wonderful their life was going to be together and she believed him.

How they had enjoyed their first time together, happy in each other's arms they cuddled for hours and just looked up to the sun and dreamed of a future.

Sitting here now, Lisa opened her eyes and didn't know whether to cry or smile when she realised the sounds of water came from the bathroom above, where Alison showered. Lisa cried.

Beth's first pink bootees sat in Lisa's hands. She remembered they were the only thing she ever knitted. It had been Margaret who taught her to knit one afternoon in her craft shop and Lisa had returned a few times to finish the pretty little things and came to know Margaret better.

There lay Beth's hospital name tag from her tiny ankle and the card from the cot showing her weight, 6lb-4oz. She was tiny and her length, Lisa couldn't quite read this anymore. It had been worn away over the years of her handling it on each of her baby's birthdays.

Lisa sat on this rug and remembered her Beth and how she came to be and how the nurse told her, sometimes these things happen for a reason; Lisa couldn't see how that had been helpful. More photos were in her hands when a knock came at her bedroom door. She scooped up her life and said, "come in."

Alison slowly opened the door and poked her head round.

"You all right?" she asked.

"Yes, I'm going to have an early night."

"Okay, I will leave you to it. Goodnight."

Alison left Lisa, but not before she had seen a wedding photo lying on the floor beside her friend. It showed Lisa in a very plain cream, knee length dress, a large floppy lace cream hat, rather like the hippies wore in the late sixties and seventies. The people next to the happy couple must have been parents, Alison guessed. But it was the other photograph that had caught her eye. Her quick look showed a man with long dark shoulder length hair and he looked remarkably like Phil. Yes, the Phil she had met that very morning.

And Lisa held another photo of herself and Phil on their wedding day. Alison had seen that one very clearly.

Although Lisa had tried to be quick and gather up her photos, now in a messy pile, she hadn't been able to hide all the faces. She wondered what Alison may have seen.

Chapter Fourteen
The Truth Will Out

Breakfast was going to be difficult. Alison wondered if she should bring up the subject of the photos. She had to; she needed to know if Phil really was Lisa's ex husband and she needed to tell Lisa she was seeing him. But was she?

They had had a coffee together, at the hospital that day. They e-mailed a lot, they had met a few times because he was now her architect but he hadn't actually asked her out on a date.

Alison made a pot of tea and a slice of toast and waited. She was getting nervous and twiddling her rings.

***

Lisa lay in bed wondering what to say when she went down to have breakfast, because she guessed Alison had seen those photos of her and Phil together.

She had also tossed other things over in her mind, like had he been lying about working on cruise ships? He must have talked to Alison online about his drawings. Surely buildings and ship drawings would be very different, she thought. Perhaps it was interior drawings he did, like the decor and layouts. Lisa was just confusing herself and decided to get showered and dressed.

***

Running down the stairs, Lisa put on a show of happiness for Alison.

"Morning," she called out bright and breezy and made a fuss of Barney. "Has Barney been out yet?" she asked.

"Yes. Tea?"

"Please." Lisa sat at the breakfast bar as Alison poured tea.

"Would you like some toast put on?" Both women were being very polite and matter of fact, all so very false and they both knew it.

"Are you feeling better this morning?" Alison asked.

"I'm fine, don't you worry about me. What are you up to today?"

"Not sure yet. Danny e-mailed me and asked me to go for lunch, once he had finished his early morning deliveries."

"That would be lovely," Lisa said. "You haven't seen him in a while, have you?"

No she hadn't but she didn't want to talk about Danny. Alison was itching to talk about those photos but how to bring it up?

"Now I have my new laptop, I've been catching up on my e-mails and Phil sent me one regarding a few more questions about the layout of my new coffee shop. Would you like to take a look?" Alison said.

Lisa said she would. She was feeling more relaxed now but it was still hard to keep her secret.

"They look really good and the colour scheme looks interesting."

"Do you know, Lisa, *my* Phil looks ever so much like that young man in your wedding photo? Older of course and his hair is much shorter now."

My Phil, how dare she think that? My Phil, indeed! Lisa was shocked at her own reaction and feelings; her back was up, and she was defensive again.

"Oh really," Lisa was trying to play it cool.

The phone rang; that gave her an excuse to drop the conversation. It was a job offer for a few days a week, for the next month.

"I have to go out and collect some paperwork on a temp job, from the agency, back soon."

Lisa left the house in a hurry, leaving Alison sitting in the kitchen thinking. She still didn't know what was going on with Lisa and now she felt dreadful because Lisa had been so good to her.

"Perhaps I'll ask Phil next time I see him," she muttered to herself.

But then again, perhaps she hadn't the nerve to ask. Alison turned her mind to what she was going to wear for her lunch date with Danny. She suddenly realised what she had thought and she said it aloud: "a lunch date."

***

As Alison left for her date, Lisa walked in with a large envelope in her hand. Alison guessed it was to do with her new job.

"You look smart, Alison."
"Have I overdone the outfit?"
"No, you look lovely."

Driving to meet Danny, Alison wondered what she was doing. She thought about her online dating adventure; it hadn't moved on any further than Phil. She hadn't been too sure about the whole idea in the first place but she gave it a go, and now she wondered if she should carry on with it. Phil and her had met but not on a date. He was nice enough but nothing exploded inside her and then she remembered Danny on that day of the coffee shop explosion. He had been her hero and she smiled to herself as a flutter rose in her middle. He made her insides explode at that moment.

She parked up and walked over to the rather posh looking Victorian restaurant in the plush hotel in town, where she saw Danny sitting at a window table. A waiter in black and white was bending over him with a bottle in his hand, wine she presumed.

Danny looked quite dashing, the closer she got and he spotted her and waved. He was dressed, it appeared from the little she could see, in a dark suit, shirt and tie. Had he been to a wedding or a funeral? Surely he wouldn't dress like that, in the middle of the day, to meet her, would he?

She had expected him to still be wearing his dark brown delivery uniform with the company logo embroidered on the pocket. She also thought they would meet at a more everyday but nice restaurant, until she received that text, earlier that morning, which made her change her outfit.

Danny stood as she walked up to his table. The waiter escorting her pulled out a chair and when she sat, he draped a large white linen napkin across her lap.

"Well this is very nice," said Alison and smiled.

"Shall we order?" he asked.

He had wanted to take her out for a very long time but hadn't liked to ask, but with the sudden realisation that she could have died, he had plucked up his courage and here they were.

Seeing each other early every morning, when he entered her coffee shop with arms full of trays holding bread and doughnuts, made it easy for both to chat and then there had been the many evening baker related events she had attended as his plus one; he had no one else to ask she had told herself.

The fact that he wasn't just a delivery driver but owned the company was a surprise to her that day.

He was a master baker but now had other people doing the work for him.

"Why choose to deliver yourself?"

She was shocked at his reply.

"So I can see you." His green eyes twinkled at her.

She blushed at this piece of information and didn't know how to answer him.

They discussed the explosion, how he would run in again to save her and how he wished he had arrived a few moments earlier and had got her out of the building before it blew up.

"Why did you come up the back fire escape to my flat?"

"When I arrived, I smelled gas and the shop door wasn't open."

"Really? I never did smell anything."

"Perhaps it had built up. I'm so sorry I pushed you into the bathroom and landed up on top of you." In different circumstances he would have enjoyed it. "I wanted to protect you, and then I heard that horrendous boom, well, I still have ringing in my ears."

"I'm sorry," Alison's pink lips gave a small smile and without thinking her hand went up to touch one of his ears.

His hand flew up to hold hers before both lowered to the table where they lay together for a moment before she pulled away.

She bent her head forward to look at her food, which she pushed around the plate with her fork; she was feeling uneasy now.

She knew she hit her head hard but remembered nothing more from that day other than the push he had given her towards her bathroom.

He explained he still felt guilty for landing on top of her, but with that boom he knew they would not get out.

"Is this what this lunch is all about? Guilt?" She wished she hadn't said that.

"No," he told her.

The subject was left and the rest of the meal was enjoyable.

Later as they left each other Danny thanked her for her company and moved forward to kiss her cheek. She accepted this and thanked him for a lovely meal and found herself saying they would have to do it again sometime.

As she walked away she felt her warm flushed cheek and smiled; she had enjoyed his touch.

***

Lisa spent the afternoon preparing for her temp work which was to start the following morning.

Her clothes were ready, pressed and co-ordinated. Shoes cleaned and matching handbag filled. She was ready, a little nervous maybe as she would be working in one of the local estate agents and fleetingly wondered if Phil would come in. Alison had mentioned he often worked with an agent in town but only ever online or by phone before her job.

So he didn't know the area, Lisa thought.

She couldn't be choosy though, she needed a job and the money that came with it. She could handle both job and Phil if need be.

***

"Hi Alison, how'd lunch go?" Lisa enquired.
"Good, thanks."

Alison went to her bedroom to change into something loose and more comfortable. She had taken her time driving back to Lisa's. She had much to think about. She had enjoyed her time with Danny and the time had passed quickly with their nonstop chatting. She hadn't realised how comfortable she felt in his presence, they had so much in common.

She was seeing him again, at the weekend and for the whole day and yes she was looking forward to it, even though he hadn't said where he was taking her.

Her whole being had shivered at the touch of his hand and she wondered why, and why had she moved to touch his ear? It wasn't premeditated and then there had been that kiss.

Having changed her clothes she left the bedroom and glanced in the mirror only to find she was smiling to herself. Thinking, how on earth did all this happen? Danny made her happy.

She went downstairs to talk some more with Lisa about both men, but there was no sign of her.

"Where's your mistress gone," she turned to Barney, who only licked her hands when she reached out to fuss him.

Moving to the kitchen she found the note left for her.

'Gone to baby sit. Sleeping over, see you tomorrow evening. Would you mind seeing to Barney, let him in and out and you know where his food is. Thanks a lot. Lisa.'

"Well Barney, looks like it's me and you. Come on here," and she bent down for a full doggie hug.

Chapter Fifteen
A Strange Lunch Date

Beth and Andy had enjoyed their first evening out together in a long time. Lisa was sound asleep by the time they arrived home from seeing a film and having dinner afterwards.

Lisa slept in the spare room which would soon become 'baby boy without a name' room.

Morning came early in Beth's house, what with a new baby screaming for his breakfast and a very excited little girl jumping all over her grandma's bed.

"Grandma, get up, come on, get up. Play with me."

Lisa would only have a little time during breakfast to play around with Lily, so instead she read a princess fairy story at the breakfast table, in return for her promise to eat all her food up.

After breakfast Lisa kissed Beth, Lily and baby goodbye and set off to work.

With a spring in her step, Lisa felt at peace with herself and the world around her. She had forgotten all about the likelihood of Phil coming into the estate agents, where she was now heading.

"Morning," she said, as she walked brightly into H. Brown and Son.

"Morning, Lisa; is it okay to call you Lisa? We're a small team here and we have quite a work load at the moment. The housing market is taking off again after the summer holidays. Would you like to start by making coffee, for my son and me and of course, yourself?"

"Yes. Thanks, Sir."

"Please, call me Harry and my boy is Ben."

Lisa smiled and went to the small kitchen tucked at the back of the shop. She was thinking she was going to like working here. She didn't always like where she was sent. Some staff looked down their noses at temps. More trouble than their worth, she had overheard at one of her placements.

It wasn't long before the phones were ringing and she was busy enjoying herself in her work. A couple came in looking for their first home together and Lisa watched them browse through the property papers she had collected together for them to choose from. They tossed aside the ones they didn't like the look of and also the ones just over their budget which Lisa had snuck in.

You never know, they might stretch themselves, if one house caught their eye, she thought; more commission.

The couple decided on three properties. It had been her with Phil who had dreamed about buying a house together many years ago.

The man coughed, to bring Lisa back from her thoughts.

"Sorry," she said and looked up from where she had noticed their hands intertwined. He asked if they could view that afternoon.

Lisa carried on with her work, and smiled at her thoughts of young love, as she arranged the times for viewings.

Lunch time came around very quickly and Lisa was just walking out of the door when Phil came rushing in. They literally bumped into each other. Her mind had been elsewhere, thinking about that couple, on the first step of owning a home together.

"Sorry. Oh, hello, what are you doing here?" Phil asked.

"Working, well, going for my lunch, actually."

Harry appeared on hearing Phil's voice.

"I'm so sorry, Harry, for being late and now I'm going to be later still," Phil said.

Harry just stood at his office door and looked at Phil with a grin.

"I'll take you to lunch," Phil said holding open the door and not giving Lisa any option. "Back soon, Harry," he said and winked at him behind Lisa's back.

Phil followed Lisa as she walked out. It was only a few yards that they walked side by side, to arrive at the cafe just around the corner, but she still felt awkward. She wondered what on earth she was doing, talking to him, let along going to have a ham roll and a cup of coffee with him.

It had all happened so suddenly. It was as though she had blinked away twenty odd years and here he was buying her her favourite ham rolls with mustard which he had remembered, when he asked what she would like.

He was in charge though, just as he had been when they were both so young. Lisa was watching him order the lunch; she was putting up her guard. He wasn't going to sweet talk her today, even though she had come here peacefully.

Yet, sitting at a table for two she still wondered if it was her that had worn him down with baby Beth, or their parents' interference, his telling him to come back home with them, saying he was too young for a wife and a baby. Or perhaps it was her parents not supporting either of them and telling Phil it was his fault entirely, that she had the baby. There he stood in the short queue wearing smart blue jeans, check shirt just showing under his waist length black leather jacket. She wondered if he still had his motorbike. For a middle aged man he wore his clothes well over a body that had been kept trim. But it must be a casual day's work, for him to dress that way she thought.

She remembered the morning he worked with Alison on her shop plans when he wore a suit, shirt and tie, and that afternoon when he bumped into her in the park he looked very smart.

Phil returned with the two drinks and went back for the plates of food.

"Hope white rolls are okay, that's all they had left." Phil set the plates down next to the glass mugs of coffee in front of her. She again looked at him, wondering if he was going to ask about that divorce again; suddenly she hoped not.

Making small talk, Phil asked about Alison and if she had liked his drawing suggestions and colours for the new coffee shop.

"I think so. She showed me. I found the colours interesting."

"Oh, what does that mean?" he asked.

"Nothing; they are just a little different to what she had before."

"That was the idea," and both decided to leave that subject alone. "Beth, how is she?" Phil asked.

"Fine without you," end of that conversation, but Beth was his daughter and he would like to know; perhaps a question for later. He intended seeing Lisa again.

"I heard your aunt died," Phil said without thinking where this statement might lead to.

"How did you know that?"

"I heard through a friend of a friend. That must have messed up things."

"What do you mean?" Lisa asked feeling annoyed.

Memories flew through her mind, mostly the money her aunt sent each month.

Lisa was furious to think he might know of this money. She had also worked hard over the years to manage. Did he think she had had it easy? She had her pride and stood up, pushed her chair back which grated along the wooden floor making other customers stop and stare. She left half of her ham roll and coffee and stormed out of the cafe and into the street.

For a split second she was disorientated, where to go? She looked left, right and felt lost. Quickly she regained her thoughts, her self respect and knew where she was going, back to H Brown and Son.

Phil wanted to cut his tongue out, kick himself, he was so irritated with her but more so with himself. He would have run after her, to grab her but he felt he shouldn't; he had tried that twice and been in trouble. Anyway he guessed where she was going, he would see her again and give his apologies, when she had calmed down.

He thought he knew her well enough, that she wouldn't make a scene at her place of work and in front of her boss. Suddenly he was unsure, perhaps she would? After all it had been a long, long time. She had changed, he had seen that; grown into an independent woman.

An hour went by before Harry asked if Mr Kingston had called back.

"No, he hasn't!" Lisa said. "Oh sorry, Mr Kingston hasn't called."

"Do you know him? Of course you both have the same name, what am I like?" And he smiled. "You're related?"

"Yes sir; he's my husband." The words just fell from her month.

Harry Brown was staggered and said no more, but returned to his office. After all, it was none of his business, but he had known Phil on and off for some years now. He and many others knew of his excellent drawings for interior design and he was well regarded in his field. He also knew he had become a very rich man through his work. But Harry knew nothing of Phil's private life and had no idea he was married. No one had ever mentioned a wife to him.

Just as the working day was ending, Phil pulled up to park outside the estate agency office. He jumped from his silver Mercedes and flew into the building like a hurricane.

Harry came out to meet him.

"I'm really late, I am so very sorry, something came up."

"Come into my office," Harry asked. "Want a drink?"

"Could do with one, but no, I'm driving. Got a coffee?" Phil looked at Lisa.

Lisa was about to leave for home, so Harry got the coffee.

"Bye, see you tomorrow," Harry called after her.

"Yes, see you at nine." Lisa was holding the door handle when she heard the start of their conversation.

"Well did you like the old house?" Harry was asking Phil as he passed him a coffee from the machine.

"Can we talk in your office please?" Phil half twisted his head to indicate that he wanted privacy.

"Yes, of course, come on in."

But it was too late; she had seen the paper Harry was holding in his hand, seen the photo of the old house lying on Harry's desk earlier that afternoon when taking in a cup of tea.

And now here was Phil buying their dream house, built on a hill, overlooking a lake and in this town where she had made her home; how dare he?

Driving home, Lisa was angry with Phil and began to think about their history.

Yes, many things had been thrown at the young pair with little money. Their life had been tough but they would have managed, Lisa was sure of that. Still, they both knew neither family would accommodate them if things went wrong.

What she didn't know was, her aunt had interfered in their life. This had brought about an almighty row leading to Phil leaving.

Lisa had cried for months after he left and that's when auntie told her to take a little of her inheritance each month while she still lived, to see her through as a single mum, rather than waiting for her to die.

In those hours when Lisa cried she kept wondering why auntie couldn't have given the money freely when Phil was with her and when she had tried to ask, auntie threatened to stop the money.

"You're best rid of him," she had said. Lisa was young and vulnerable with a baby and didn't ask again.

Little did Lisa know that Phil hadn't wanted to leave but had felt pressured into it, for the sake of his wife and baby.

Phil left, but he was to get nothing, all monies went to Lisa. It had been her mother, only a few years ago, at her aunt's funeral, who had told Lisa of this arrangement.

It was then that Lisa realised it was all her family's doing, but why was her Phil so weak? Why hadn't he stood up to her family, turned the money down?

Lisa had felt confused then and again now, she felt she could scream, but at who? Her mother or her dead aunt, rather late for that, she thought; Phil, yes, she wanted to scream at Phil.

Suddenly Lisa changed her mind about going home and turned off the main road and drove to visit little Lily instead. She always made her grandma feel happy and at that moment she didn't really know how she felt. Her mind was all over the place.

"Hi mum, this is a nice surprise, come on in, want a cupper?" Beth was always pleased to see Lisa.

Lily came running up to hug her knees and shouted, "grandma, grandma, come and play with me."

"Leave grandma alone, she's tired after work," Beth said to her little girl.

"Oh, she's all right," and Lisa took hold of Lily's little hand. She followed Lily through to her play area at the end of the sitting room and sat on the floor.

"Here's your tea," Beth said, passing her mother a rose patterned china mug. "Are you okay?" she asked.

"Yes, of course I am. Can't I just drop in to see my lovely family?" But Beth noticed how her mum frowned and looked down as she took her tea. Beth still felt there was some underlying reason for her visit.

"Will you stop for dinner? Andy will be back soon, he's just popped down the shops for me."

"That would be nice, but I had better get back. I just wanted a cuddle with my Lily," and hearing that Lily ran to jump on Lisa again.

"I love you grandma," she said with a beaming smile building on her fair, sweet face, that of an innocent child. Lisa hugged her two girls, as she called them and looked in on a peaceful, sleeping baby before she left.

"I'll be off. See you soon, take care." And Lisa left Beth wondering what was going on with her mother.

Andy arrived home with the shopping which, for once, he got right, or so Beth told him. Mind, there was only half a dozen things to get.

"Mum's been round."

"Oh, what did she want?" He didn't mean it the way it sounded, he quite liked Lisa nowadays.

"I'm really not sure. There's something going on with her and I just can't put my finger on it."

"Why don't you take an evening off? I'll baby sit and you take a bottle of wine and have a chat with your mum."

"Yes, I will arrange it for when Alison is out."

The next day Beth did just that and Lisa was pleasantly pleased to think she would have her daughter all to herself, something which didn't happen so much these days.

"How about Friday?" asked Lisa.

She knew Alison had said she was to meet her architect, to discuss her new coffee shop details, but over dinner. Really?

Lisa was convinced something more was going on there with Alison and Phil. She was glad Beth was coming round because it would stop her thinking about them together.

She wondered why it bothered her, but it did.

Chapter Sixteen
Dinner Date

Friday came around and Alison was getting changed for her date with the architect as she liked to call him in front of Lisa. She felt sure that using Phil's name was hurtful to her.

As Alison left, Beth arrived. Both were using taxis, as they were aware they would be drinking that evening. They were using wine for Dutch courage, Alison because she wanted to ask Phil questions regarding Lisa and Beth was going to ask her mother what or who was causing her stress.

Wine corks popped in two very different places, but with people who were connected and with similar thoughts and questions.

***

"Are you well, Alison?" Phil asked as they sat just over from where she had sat only ten days before with Danny, for that enjoyable lunch.

"Yes, fine and looking forward to seeing the finished drawings you have to show me. Are we any nearer to a date to start building?"

Alison was getting tired of all the red tape she had to go through, to start her life again. There had been a coffee shop standing on that spot for over a hundred years, so why was planning permission required? The council should just get on with it, she explained to Phil.

"Why? Are you tired of living at Lisa's?" he enquired.

"Well, no, not really, but I sense there is something going on with you two and I feel awkward about it."

Phil took a moment before answering.

"Yes there is, and?" but before Phil could say anything more the waiter returned to take their orders and quickly left again. "Now where were we? Oh yes; is there a problem with us meeting?"

The waiter had left but would soon return. Alison avoided answering, lowered her eyes and smiled before taking a sip of her Prosecco.

"Here, let me show you a few sketches, before plates take over our table." He pulled a folder from his man bag to change the subject.

Alison was very impressed with what she was shown and agreed to everything.

"How long before they start?" She asked. "What was the company's name again?"

"Standford, are the builders and Mayson the decorators," he told her. "Not long, perhaps a few weeks, a couple of months; maybe a little longer to finish up." She was pleased with the outcome and was smiling at him.

Their main meal arrived. They had skipped a starter to leave room for a pudding.

"Hey slow down on the wine," Phil laughed. He thought he might have to carry her home.

"Look, I need to ask you something personal and I don't know how to." She hoped the Prosecco might have helped.

"That sounds ominous," he said, only guessing at what it might be.

She took another mouthful of bubbles and was ready to ask her question when the waiter reappeared to remove their plates. She sat back from the table and let him do his work, then leant forward to speak, but like lightning the waiter returned with the dessert menu which he was placing in their hands.

Alison held her breath, she was becoming frustrated.

"This looks delicious; I'll have the raspberry cheesecake," Alison said.

"And I'll have the chocolate profiteroles," Phil told the waiter who quickly left, taking the menus with him.

This had given her a little more time to think what she was going to say.

"Now, young lady, what's your problem?"

Alison laughed. This was all madness to her. She hadn't been called young in years and a lady too, or was he being condescending with that look on his face?

"Well it's, yeah, it's..." and Phil raised an eyebrow at her. "Well, it's Lisa and you."

"I see," and the waiter was back as Phil sat back in his chair.

Oh, for god's sake will I ever get this out?

"This looks fantastic," he said looking down on his dish and then he smiled up at Alison.

"Stop it, stop playing with me." Alison was getting irritated and wanted to throw her first spoonful of cheesecake at him, but what a waste that would have been.

"I'm sorry; Lisa is my wife."

Alison dropped her next spoonful of cheesecake and her dessert fork too. The cutlery hit the china plate with a clang drawing the attention of the couple at the next table.

"You fond of dating women, when you're already married, are you?" Alison said rather loudly and glared at that couple, who then turned their heads away.

"It's not like that and who said this was a date anyway? I thought it was about the coffee shop?"

Oh dear, Phil knew that sounded bad. Now he felt he had hurt her feelings; he seemed to be doing that all the time these days. Yes he had found her on a *'finding love, dating line'* and he had been e-mailing her back and forth, but then, there had been no Lisa on his radar.

"Sorry. I meant to say, I asked Lisa for a divorce, once I realised there was no hope there, what with her having a partner."

"What partner?" Alison didn't understand. "Were you going to ask her for a divorce before the online thing, or since you met me, Phil?"

The well dressed older woman, of the couple at the next table held her hand up to the side of her face; she was obviously saying something to the bald headed man she was with.

Phil lowered his voice.

"When I first went online, I was only looking for a woman's company and didn't quite know where it might lead." He lied to save her feelings. Alison wasn't to know he hadn't written to Lisa, to ask for a divorce before,.

What was she asking him? This conversation was getting totally out of hand; there was going to be no winner here and all they were doing was digging deeper holes for themselves.

Alison stood up sharply and pushed her chair back as a waiter dashed over to help.

"I think it's time I left, don't you?" She said sharply.

"Finish your dessert," Phil said calmly looking around the room.

No, she wouldn't do that, taking no notice of a full restaurant. She hadn't lowered her voice.

"Leave any other drawing or information at the Browns. I'll collect them from there."

She left, with a little wobble on her Prosecco filled legs.

Phil was left, sitting alone at a table for the second time in a week by two totally different women, both leaving their half eaten food.

Phil paid for the meal with his bank card and the waiter thanked him for the generous tip while, as Phil saw it, giving a knowing grin; he must have seen some things during his time waiting tables.

Phil replaced his wallet in his back pocket and stood to leave. He glanced across at the older couple and smiling, remarking: "I hope we kept you entertained this evening."

He didn't stop for a reply. He hoped they were as embarrassed as he was.

***

On arriving home, Alison almost fell in the door and again passed Beth who was just leaving and even in her rather tipsy state, Alison noticed Beth had been crying and Lisa too. Alison plonked herself down in the chair opposite Lisa who took up the whole of the sofa, legs flung up and over the arms. Too much wine for Lisa as well, Alison thought.

What an evening the three women had had.

"Coffee?" Lisa suggested and struggled to her feet.

Holding onto the back of the sofa she felt her way along to then touch the wall leading to the kitchen.

"Please," Alison shouted after her.

Quite soon the two women sat with their coffees and the earlier wine must have loosened them up, because the conversation flowed so easily. Talk of life and what it throws at people and how they react to it carried on well into the early hours.

Lisa explained about her young marriage and who Phil really was, without Alison interrupting her.

They wondered why he was back. Was it for a divorce?

Lisa still held the lifelong love for a man she thought didn't want her anymore. She also told Alison that she had finally told Beth that evening who Phil was.

Beth had almost collapsed with a mixture of disbelief and excitement because she might perhaps now meet her father and get to know him; have a grandfather for her children, and then the reality struck home. How could he come back after all this time and ask for a divorce, to gain his freedom and hurt her mother all over again?

Beth had gone home feeling frustrated and really angry at that man. After an evening like this the three women would all have a bad head in the morning, and all because of one man.

Beth cried but couldn't tell Andy why for a good few days. That made him angry.

Alison was angry at a man who wasn't free to date her.

And Lisa cried because she didn't want a divorce and was angry at herself for still wanting Phil.

And Danny; had Alison forgotten the kindness, even the love that he had shown her?

***

Once Beth felt able to tell Andy about her father staying so close, he asked what she was going to do about it.

She really didn't know. Her instincts were that she loved him because he was her father but he hadn't earned her love, to be her dad, had he?

Beth knew she had a nice little nest egg of money stashed away because of him but it wasn't about the money. It was because she hadn't told Andy about it and that could come between them, if he knew she had been keeping secrets.

They could have used that money when setting up home together and having their babies, when money was really tight.

What a mess, she thought, and then not so much a mess for her, but for her mum.

***

No one had seen Phil for a couple of weeks. Lisa was asked by Harry whether she had had contact, as he had papers for him to sign off on a property he was buying. No she hadn't.

This property information, Lisa just couldn't fathom. Why would he be buying a house around here?

Then Harry had to dash off one late afternoon to meet a client. He asked if she could lock up for him. Lisa grabbed her opportunity to look into his filing cabinet. Turning off the display lights beaming down on the boards holding pictures of houses and flats in the windows, she moved quickly to his office where the filing cabinet key hung from its lock.

She took a look around, no one could see her. The front door was locked and no one could enter, or so she thought.

Fingering through the files for properties sold subject to contract she came across, *Kingston*. Another quick look around Harry's office and she pulled the file from its section, opened it and there was Phil's name. Further down the page a photo of their teenage dream house, to her it seemed a small mansion. The shock of reading the price made her drop a couple of pages and then she thought she heard the front door opening. She rushed to pick up the papers. Quickly put the paperwork back together and replaced the file, shut the cabinet drawer and was turning the key just as Ben walked in.

"What are you doing?" he asked sharply.

Lisa stumbled over her words in fright.

"Hello Ben. Your father hadn't locked the files away, so I was just doing it for him, as he asked me to lock up the place. He's out, had a late appointment."

Ben wasn't sure he believed her and took the keys from her hands to finish the job. He bade her goodnight and Lisa left.

Ben could be short with her sometimes and she hoped that was the reason and no other.

All the way home Lisa wondered at the purchase Phil was making. Why that house? The one they had dreamed of buying when they were so young and in love and had dreamed a fantasy. Back then they knew they would never be able to buy such a place. But how could he now? Was Phil trying to rub salt into her wounds? She didn't like him at that moment. She thought of what could have been, and a single tear found its way from the corner of her eye. She had to stop this crying, she was a grown woman.

Lisa arrived home just as Alison did and Beth too.

"I have a welcoming committee," Lisa commented and discreetly wiped at her eyes in case they still glistened. She had always been good at covering her feelings.

All three smiled at each other as they entered the house. Something was going on; she could feel it in the air.

"I have news," Beth said.

"Me too," Alison said.

"Wow, you had both better come into the kitchen then."

Congregating around the breakfast bar, Lisa put the kettle on. Alison grabbed three mugs from the mug tree and Beth held the tin of tea bags.

"Well, come on. Who's going to tell me first?" Lisa asked, looking from one to the other.

"Go on Alison, you go." Beth was bursting to tell but wanted to be last.

"Well, I have a finishing date for the building and once the painter has done his work and the new furniture is delivered, I shall be moving within a couple of weeks after that, just in time for the Christmas rush. What a boost that will be, what with so many people out and about Christmas shopping."

"That's great news, but I will miss having you here," Lisa said and thought how quickly time had passed.

"And you, Beth, what's your news? Not pregnant again so soon are we?" Alison joked and laughed.

"Well." Beth grinned.

Her mother's face was a picture. Shock! Horror! Baby with no name would have a sibling almost the same age as him.

"No! You're not?" Lisa said.

"No, just fooling with you."

"You have a name for baby?" Lisa's eyes brightened.

"No, will you both shut up and listen." Beth was busting to tell.

Lisa and Alison both took sips of tea and Beth waited for them to put their mugs down.

"I'm getting married." And she punched the air with her fist, she was so very happy. It had taken Andy ten years to set the date. Of course the engagement took place in that old coffee shop five years ago and in front of many people.

"What? Oh darling, at last, that's wonderful." Lisa hugged her daughter and Alison joined them. A huddle of women in the middle of the kitchen and Barney jumped up to join them.

"When, where, have you fixed a date?" Lisa wanted to know all the details.

"Christmas Eve; Andy came up with the idea and I just loved it."

"That will be so pretty, with all the decorations up and a glittering tree too. Perhaps it will snow, a white wedding, maybe." Lisa was so very excited that she forgot all about Phil and his big house, until Beth dropped another bombshell.

"I want my father to give me away." She stood perfectly still and waited for a reaction from her mother. Lisa went pale and quiet before she took another mouthful of tea.

Beth looked at Alison who said nothing. Had she to ask her mother again?

"Do you really mind, mum? He is my dad after all and he has never forgotten me; remember the money twice a year? He never forgot the date of my birthday or Christmas." She felt she had to remind her mum of something Lisa knew only too well.

Lisa looked into her tea, thinking what she could

say. She knew Beth was right.

"He is your father. I'm not sure I would call him your dad. And no, he hasn't ever forgotten you, but money cannot buy love and you don't really know him."

"I know all that, but it's what Andy and I most want. The wedding will only be a small affair."

She was thinking it wouldn't be too awkward to explain to a few friends who Phil was, if the need arose.

Then Beth turned again to look at Alison with those pleading eyes of hers and asked:

"Could we hold the reception in your new coffee shop, Alison?"

"Oh, yes that would be lovely," and instinctively beamed from ear to ear but then wondered how Lisa would feel about it.

"If that's okay with your mum." Alison turned to look at Lisa, who still wore her serious face.

"What can I say; as long as you're sure everyone is happy with the arrangements, then its fine by me. Two things though. You have to ask your father and have you told Andy about the money saved for a wedding?"

It was a no to both Lisa's questions. Calmly Lisa told Beth to sort both issues out herself. She was having no dealings with either and especially with her father and she drank her tea.

Beth had already planned it in her head. She would have her father over to her house, introduce Andy and her children and try to get to know him a little.

Alison was very excited at holding a wedding reception at her brand spanking new coffee house. She had decided to call it Alison's Coffee House, not just, 'Alison's coffees,' as it had been and she thought 'House' gave it a little more distinction.

Beth thanked Alison and said she would be back to discuss the arrangements. Then she moved towards her mother and wrapped her arms around her. Lisa whispered, "I love you; be happy."

Chapter Seventeen
Christmas

Christmas Eve arrived; Lily was dressed as a Princess, in pale pink, her favourite colour. The bride was as pretty as a picture in white chiffon, over a net skirt, with a pink silk top to match Lily's dress and baby was in pale blue silk trousers, with a sweet white silk shirt.

Both girls had a tiara in their hair, no veil for Beth but there was a tiny one for Lily and it sparkled as she kept telling anyone who would listen.

It was a registry office wedding. Andy waited inside a small green room where cream covered chairs formed a semi-circle. Lisa stood beside him and held the baby.

Danny sat between Alison and Margaret, who had just walked in to sit behind Lisa. Margaret wore a dark blue two piece suit with a pink blouse, dark blue shoes and handbag, with a small blue and pink netting box shaped hat, the size of a fascinator; it toppled to the side of her head as she fiddled with it.

"Love the big hat," Margaret said to Alison as she arrived wearing a bold red hat trimmed with white imitation fur.

Was Margaret being kind or was she using her usual sharp tongue?

"I love the hat." Lisa turned to Alison and winked. She had heard Margaret's comment.

"It's just right for Christmas and matches your

red dress." Lisa thought it quite novel really, remembering the outfit she wore to a wedding some five years ago; back than Jack and Rosie had mentioned Alison's coffee and cream suit and marshmallow looking hat and Lisa had heard. Now Father Christmas would spring to their minds when they saw this outfit, Lisa was sure of that. Of course neither one would reveal their comments to Alison.

Jack and Rosie were always larking about, whether out socially or at work in the hospital.

Lisa, the proud mother of the bride, looked wonderful in her red and green tartan taffeta full skirt, finished with a red silk blouse. To keep the theme, her hat was small and green with a sprig of Holly and red berries attached to it.

Andy's parents were a little more reserved. His mother wore a cream suit and gold blouse while his father dressed in a dark blue, almost black suit.

Beth had wanted a Christmas theme and that's just what she got, even down to the women wearing silly Christmas earrings, the bigger the better and some even lit up; Lily loved those. Beth wished for a fun time and it was fun, nothing like any other wedding anybody could remember.

With two children and having lived with Andy for a few years, she didn't want the big white wedding thing, so she had already spoken to Phil about the money he had always sent her. She asked if he would be okay with her using some of it to reduce their mortgage and some for her wedding day, keeping a small amount back for a rainy day. He thought his daughter very wise and realised Lisa had made a good job of raising her.

Of course he was happy with that and Andy was delighted to not have to worry about the cost of a wedding, now he knew of the money.

The music played and the bride arrived looking stunning on her father's arm, him in a grey suit with a silver waistcoat, a pink shirt and grey tie. He did her justice.

"He's quite a catch," Margaret said to Alison as both looked at Phil.

"Margaret," Alison said, surprised at the older woman's comment but she wasn't sure she wanted to catch him anymore. Margaret had a feeling she never would.

The grey suit picked out the little grey in his dark hair, Lisa thought as she watched father and daughter walking together, a sight she had never expected to see.

Lisa had to admire him for sending the money, to make this day happen; she wouldn't have ever afforded it, but wished Beth hadn't missed out on all those years of having a proper dad about the house.

He was handsome. The years had been kind to him and yes, her eyes still showed her love for him which had never died. She had to look away as happy tears filled those eyes.

Beth turned to her mother as she walked by and noticed those eyes; she smiled and mouthed a few words to Lisa. *Mum, be happy.* Lisa understood what she meant.

The service was over. Beth and Andy were married and it was such a happy time. Lisa took

Phil's arm to walk behind the bride and groom and it made her quiver inside. He smiled that unforgettable smile at her. "You all right?" he asked.

He saw her eyes full of tears and felt the way she clung to his arm. Her touch made him realise how much he had missed her closeness.

"Just very happy," Lisa said and smiled at him while she squeezed his arm a little tighter.

Lisa didn't really know Andy's parents and they were happy enough walking together at the back of this small group of people. The main guests were waiting in the coffee house.

Alison took hold of Danny's arm and followed on. She had been seeing him on and off over the lead up to the wedding, albeit much of the time was spent sorting out cake and bread requirements for that day and before that, for the grand opening of her coffee house.

They had often lunched together when the business side of things was nearing completion and she found she was rather fond of him and missed him when he left.

Margaret took hold of Lily's hand. After all she had visited Beth a few times since baby arrived and knew Lily well; not that she would ever let on she enjoyed playing little girl games. She also pushed the buggy now containing the baby.

Alison had left Becky, Joe and Mia in charge of entertaining the people not attending the actual marriage. Judging by the sound of laughter coming from the opened doors as the main guests arrived, they had succeeded.

The place was decked out in white, red and green, for a wedding with a Christmas look.

The coffee house was a dream picture for the bride and groom when they arrived to be covered in confetti. The wedding cake was a mountain of cup cakes with different coloured icing with either an icing sugar Christmas tree or a sprig of holly sat on top of each one.

A huge ring of mixed doughnuts spread around the base of the stand and on the very top of this strange arrangement stood a Father Christmas holding hands with a Christmas Fairy. Their faces had small pictures of Andy and Beth stuck on to them.

It was all a bit tacky but everyone took it at face value and laughed and that was the whole point.

There were finger foods of all types laid on Christmas platters on tables arranged around the room. Guests moved from table to table to greet and chat with each other; pulling chairs into groups.

Rosie was in her element when walking up to the cake stand and seeing what there was to eat. Her enormous smile appeared; she was in Heaven.

Jack the paramedic was talking to Alison and admiring her hat.

Mollie with her tiny bump hidden under a white flowing blouse with a holly and ivy corsage pinned to it, walked over to Beth, to wish her well.

"Mollie, you never phoned to tell me, congratulations; when's it due?" Beth hugged her.

The two of them had become very good friends since that stormy day when they first met in the department store, wearing raincoats of the same style.

But with Mollie living away, Beth hadn't seen her too often, perhaps only once a year.

"I have more news too, Beth. I am moving just an hour's drive away, in the new year."

"That's great. Your bump will grow and then can play with my two. Do you know what it is yet?"

"I don't want to know. I don't want to miss out on the excitement as it arrives."

Both girls laughed together when carrying on their conversation.

"What's so funny?" Andy said as he walked up to place his arm around his new wife.

"Nothing, just girl talk," Mollie said and patted her bump to show him before Beth had a chance to say.

There was one thing bothering Mollie though; she would be living nearer to her mother, Margaret, and they didn't always see eye to eye.

Michael was talking to Paul, who was still unattached. Far too busy being the hospital's best surgeon, people around him said. Rosie added as she walked up: "he has loads of admirers you know. I'm one but he doesn't look my way."

Grace and Josh arrived late as they got stuck in bad weather. Beth and Mollie were pleased to see them arrive safely. It had been a long time since all three women had been together. In fact it had been five years. Josh was climbing the ladder of success in the police force; Grace was pleased to tell them all.

Beth hadn't liked to ask Grace about children and she hadn't been forthcoming with any information on that score. So she presumed there were none and perhaps she didn't want children, not everyone does, or maybe it just hadn't happened and that would be sad for them. There were a few more of Beth's work colleagues from the hospital there too, along with Andy's new boss and others from the sweet factory, where he was now chief buyer. Beth was pleased about this because he wouldn't be driving long distances anymore as sales reps do. He would be home with her and the children at a reasonable time and that made her and Lisa happy.

Andy's parents had taken to Beth, although at first they had concerns about her young age at only nineteen when first setting up home with their son.

Everyone was mingling well and chatting while Christmas music played in the background. Red and green Christmas baubles with the guest names written on in white hung on the Christmas tree standing just inside the door, one for each guest to take home as mementoes of Beth and Andy's wedding day.

The newlyweds hoped their friends would bring these baubles out each year and hang them on their own trees, to remember this, their wonderful day.

Mia, Becky and Joe now helped to serve Champagne, while Alison made Margaret's tea which she requested, of course, and by the end of the day many were drinking coffee with shots of every kind.

The day went exceptionally well and Lisa avoided any confrontation with Phil and actually danced in his arms. A short time into that dance she had closed her eyes and daydreamed as he slowly moved her around. She didn't want the music to ever stop. At the end he kissed her neck and she opened her eyes, smiled and stepped away.

He felt a little lost. Suddenly he realised what family and friends were all about, what with everyone knowing each other and he wanted some of that.

Margaret chatted for a long time with Phil, as Alison, the only other person he knew well enough to talk to was taken up with Danny and the bride and groom were conversing with everyone.

As the last guests left, Beth went to hug Lisa to thank her, not only for the wedding but for all she had done for her during her life. She whispered, "*be happy,* I love you mum," and began to walked away.

"Yes darling and I love you too, always have, always will."

Beth took a step back.

"Mum, I have one last request of you." Dare she ask, she hesitated.

"Anything," Lisa looked at her.

"I want to call baby, Lee Philip, after you and dad."

"Oh!" a second or two passed after her short breath. What could Lisa say? She smiled at Beth. "That's a lovely idea," and she kissed her daughter's cheek, the one with the dimple, just like her father's.

Phil looked over just at that moment and he knew Lisa was okay with the baby's name. Beth had already asked him if he thought her mother would mind. He hadn't been sure.

Phil looked on and as the newlyweds went to leave he followed them to the door and wished them well. To his delight Beth turned and kissed his cheek.

"Thanks for being here, Dad."

The day finished, as it began, a happy day for the couple who were married at last and the baby smiled when he was told his name, only he was too young to understand.

When it was all over Lisa took her grandchildren back to her house, so the newlyweds could have a peaceful night's sleep in their own bed. Margaret smiled at Lisa when she relayed that information to her.

The children would be sleeping in Alison's old room as she had moved back above the coffee house.

Lisa looked forward to a noisy breakfast for a change. Phil escorted Margaret home and Alison locked up, leaving the mess till morning.

She walked up her stairs, to her grand new modern flat, above her fantastic ultra modern coffee house with the new gas cookers. Danny was holding her arm as she walked in a carefree way. At last she had found her love which had always been there, she just hadn't seen it. Arriving inside her flat she threw a knowing glance at Danny, took his hand and led him in; tonight would not only be Beth and Andy's night, but hers and Danny's too.

Chapter Eighteen
Life Moved On

It was the third week of January when Lisa was asked back to work for Harry at the estate agents.

Walking in that morning, she remembered the huge house Phil was buying. She drove past it quite often and it still stood empty, even though there was a sold board outside. She hadn't seen or heard from Phil since the wedding.

Perhaps she would ask Harry about that sale, but not when Ben was within earshot. She remembered that evening she locked up.

"Morning, had a good New Year?" Harry asked Lisa as she walked in.

"Yes thanks, coffee before we start?" She said.

"That would be good," and Harry went to his office.

"Me too," a voice said, as the door opened behind her.

It was Ben striding through the door. Now she couldn't ask Harry about that house sale.

"Don't forget me," another voice came.

She recognised that voice and remembered the heartfelt and funny speech it had given at the wedding.

Still with her back to the voice, Lisa knew it was Phil and thought, *there's a fantastic new coffee house opened down the road.* She would have loved to have said this aloud but he was an important client, even if they did have history. What was he doing here? She had half hoped he wouldn't come in and yet knew he would one day. She turned to pass his drink to him.

"Harry, fancy a spot of lunch? I have a few drawings I would like you to look over and discuss with you." Phil had left Lisa's side and she was pleased to be free to work.

"Yes; won't be a minute, just need to finish up here," Harry said.

"Happy New year Lisa," Phil said and followed Harry into his office.

"And to you," she replied keeping her head down at her work.

He was unsettling her again. Phil reappeared from the back office and moved nearer to her as he waited for Harry to put his coat on.

Lisa felt very uncomfortable with him so close. She had enjoyed that dance and wished for a reason to replay it; well, part of her did, yet she knew it was the magic of the day she had been caught up in.

"Actually, I was wondering if you would have dinner with me tonight. I need to talk to you about something very important."

Before Lisa could reply and say no, Harry had Phil by the arm, "come on then, let's be off."

And Harry led Phil out of the building.

"By the way, Ben said you can leave early, just cover over the lunch time and then feel free to go."

"Thanks Harry," Lisa said and smiled at him as he left.

"I'll pick you up at seven thirty," Phil said and was gone, shutting the door behind him.

"Hey, wait just a minute."

But the two men were out of the door and getting into Phil's car. She could do nothing but think about what he had just said; dinner, tonight.

What was she to do about Phil? She had made a New Year resolution that her life was fine as it was and not to change it.

She thought leaving early would be good, because Ben always saved the chores for her. Not that she would ever complain, just in case he brought that evening up. She didn't want to discuss that as she had never been a convincing liar. At six foot six, Ben towered above her, a mere five foot four; she always felt uneasy around him.

He was good looking with his well built frame, blue eyes and short cut blonde hair, only he knew it and marched around full of his own importance. He was so very different to his father but the one time Lisa had met Ben's mother she knew exactly where his attitude came from.

The rest of the morning went slowly. She was continually looking at the clock. Phil said he would pick her up at seven thirty and she wondered if she should go. What to wear, not too smart, don't look as though you're trying too hard, girl. But not too casual either.

Two o'clock came and Ben was back from lunch.

"You may go now," he said, looking down his nose at her.

She was very happy to leave.

It was late afternoon and Lisa was pulling garment after garment out of her wardrobe, trying them on and then discarding the outfit. Clothes were piling up on her bed, shoes lay at angles strewn across the floor.

She wanted to look her best, even show off her figure which she had worked so hard to regain after she had let herself go some five years ago.

She checked her hair roots for grey, but couldn't see any growth. It hadn't been long since she'd had it coloured.

In a man, it was said he looked distinguished, in a woman it showed her age; this always annoyed her.

By six she was showered and underwear was on, a pretty pink and lacy matching set. Why these, she thought, after all, he wasn't going to see them, was he? But she admired herself in the full length mirror anyway.

'Not too bad for a forty three year old,' she thought.

By the time seven o'clock arrived Lisa had her make-up on, perfume filled the air and she was marching up and down in her flimsy blue silk dressing gown.

Whatever was the matter with her? *I'm a grown woman, a mother for god's sake, a grandmother to two.* She suddenly despaired of herself.

"I must pull myself together," she said aloud.

She finished dressing, turned to Barney and asked him if she looked okay. Barney barked nicely back at her, as if to say 'you'll do'.

A knock at the door, he was here, early. Lisa grabbed a gulp of air and then slowly let it flow out.

She smoothed her tight black dress down her

body to her knees, checked her face and earrings in the hall mirror. With her finger and thumb she felt the long gold chain which fell into the deep V of her dress, showing just the smallest amount of cleavage. She walked unsteadily in her stilettos to the door, twisted its round brass handle and stood before him.

"Hello, please come in," she said politely, now in control of herself.

It was Phil who felt uneasy now, uncomfortable, awkward, all those things, because this was the first time he had set foot in this house since he allowed her aunt to persuade him to leave, made it difficult for him to stay. She smelled delightful, tempting even and she looked even better. He allowed his eyes to run over her and cursed himself for ever leaving her. His heart was beating faster. This woman standing before him was lovelier than any woman he had ever had on his arm. No one had ever come close to his Lisa.

"I'm ready, where are we going?" she asked, whilst picking up her deep red coat and noticing how dashing he looked in his open neck, pale blue shirt and dark suit.

"I thought we would go to the little pub in the village, just off the main road."

"Okay, fine."

Lisa thought, now I'm over dressed. She was ready for somewhere a little more up market.

He opened the car door for her and she noticed the expensive grey leather seats, the smell of a new car. Some demon inside her wondered if he had hired it for the evening, just to impress her, but no, she remembered it parked outside H Browns. She pushed the thought away; if he could afford that house, he could certainly afford a prestige car.

Little was said. A few words were spoken about Beth's wedding and how he was in awe at being a grandfather.

Then suddenly Lisa blurted out what she had heard at work, that he had bought the house on the hill. As soon as she mentioned it, she felt she shouldn't have. Confidentiality was an important part of her job. But she was sad they hadn't lived their dream in that house.

"Yes, that's right. It needs an awful lot of renovating."

"That sounds like an expensive project," Lisa said.

"That's true," he replied.

She was intrigued to know what it was like inside. She would love to see the old place but wasn't going to tell him that. After all, it was their dream when they were teenagers to have it as their home, but now she didn't really want to remember; or did she?

"Those were the drawings I was showing Harry when we went to lunch. Later that afternoon he came up to the old place with me, to see how they could work."

"I see," Lisa said.

"Would you like to see? I'll take you there, now if you want." Phil didn't wait for an answer and turned off the main road they were on, to head up a dark twisting lane of hedgerows and old trees.

Lisa couldn't say anything, it was too late. They were there sitting in his smart car outside a tumbling down old house. Perhaps that was just a little bit of an exaggeration in Lisa's mind. The brick work looked sound but the old wooden window frames and door were in need of replacing. It wasn't tumbling down, far from it.

Phil got out of the car and went round to open her door but Lisa was already out and slammed her door shut behind her. She would show him she was independent.

She followed him around the outside of the house; they both peered through the windows but it was too dark to see in. She stood and tried to survey the extensive gardens he said it had, but this was January; she couldn't see any distance.

A vision went through her mind, as to what she could do with a garden that size and how her grandchildren would love the space to play in.

"I have the keys but there is no electric and the floorboards aren't safe," Phil told her.

Lisa felt interested but sad at the same time and wanted to leave. She had so wanted that dream and it couldn't be. They would never have had that sort of money to spend on a house of such size and style which led Lisa to wonder how he could afford to buy it now and this car too.

"Can we go?" she said as she turned back to the car.

Phil couldn't quite make out her voice, it was quiet and soft, even a touch of sadness clung to the words.

"Yes of course."

***

Their dinner went well in the George and Dragon pub on the green. It wasn't too crowded; the food was good and hot. And both chatted freely and nothing more was said about a divorce. They did mention bumping into Danny and Alison, who were leaving the pub as they arrived.

"That was a surprise, seeing them two here, together and holding hands, did you notice that?" Lisa pointed out.

"Perhaps they thought no one would be out here, who would know them," Phil added.

"Maybe you have lost out there," Lisa replied.

"Or perhaps Alison has given up with online dating altogether? She may even think my heart lies elsewhere."

Phil waited for a reaction from Lisa, only what he got was her telling him, she needed to go home.

Phil settled the bill and waited for Lisa to return from the toilet. She took her time; she was trying to clear her head as she stared at herself in the small mirror above the wash hand basin.

She had been wined and dined after seeing the old house and was totally confused. With a deep breath she walked out, thinking no man was going to muddle with her brain and especially not one named Phil.

The drive back to her home was quiet. Phil walked her to her door. It was a cold night and she shivered with the door key in her hand. But was that shiver due to the cold?

"You're cold, you had better go in," Phil said, taking the key from her hand which he brushed and felt her tremble. He unlocked for her and returned the key as she pushed the door open.

Lisa hesitated, wondering if she should ask him in. No. She would never ask him in.

She wasn't changing her life.

She said thanks for an interesting evening and wished him well with the house buying. In fact she repeated herself to make her point.

"I hope all goes well with the house. Goodnight." and she was through the door and shut it behind her before he could say another word.

He had hoped to kiss her goodnight.

She leaned on the door, knowing full well he was still standing on the other side. She waited. She half wondered if he would knock; he didn't. Time seemed to stand still before she heard his car pull away and then she moved and collapsed on her sofa, still in her coat with Barney close by her feet. His head soon found her lap and she stoked him around his ears.

"Oh, Barney! What am I going to do?"

As Phil drove to his hotel room he was wondering what plan he could come up with to win her heart back and have the love of his life with him, in that house, their dream house, together into old age.

***

Lisa lay fully clothed on her bed now and was still staring up at the ceiling by the time Phil arrived back at his hotel.

"What now?" she asked herself aloud. "I want him; no, I need him."

He lay on his bed, also looking up; he loved her and wanted her back as his wife.

Chapter Nineteen
A Dream

Lisa seemed to be working permanently for H. Brown and Sons these days. Apparently Harry had asked the temping agency to send her. He liked the way she worked. They had become a good team and he liked Lisa, even if Ben had made it clear to his father he wasn't so sure.

Lisa didn't mind as she knew her way around the office and also liked Harry; he had become her father figure.

Phil often popped in to see Harry and on the odd occasion he took her to lunch and she could cope with that, just. But he hadn't asked her out to dinner again; she wondered why.

She still wasn't keen on Ben but he was mostly out showing clients around houses, so she coped with him too.

One day when they were extra busy, Harry asked if she would go with Phil to the planning offices to take notes. Harry was snowed under with paperwork, or so he said. The end of the financial year was looming and she had seen how his papers were mounting up on his desk.

Lisa felt she had no choice but to go and went with notebook and pen in her handbag. After the meeting, which went in Phil's favour, they had lunch together. He wanted to celebrate having his plans passed for the changes to that old house. When she found out what the plans were she was determined not to ask to see them. She really didn't want to show any interest in them whatsoever and had she known, she would have protested; or would she?

Phil had asked Harry if he could arrange for her to go with him. He wanted her there, to be part of his future; he was planning and hoping.

"This is becoming a habit," he said "You coming for lunch with me."

She only smiled at him, not wanting to get drawn into anything more.

The situation was all very relaxed and getting into Phil's car, he asked if she would like to see the old house in daylight. It had been a few weeks since they had visited in the dark when they went to the George and Dragon pub.

"I don't think so. I have to be back at work." Lisa felt scared at the thought of going inside her dream house, especially with him.

"Look, I'll phone Harry. I'm sure with all the business I put his way he won't mind me taking you off for another hour."

Phil was talking to Harry before she had the chance to refuse. She was letting him decide for her again but felt if she had wanted to say no, she could have and wondered why she hadn't.

"Great, we won't be too long." And Phil clicked off his mobile phone. "Right, come on. Let's go."

It was a pretty drive now at the end of March. The daffodils were out and the sun was shining. Lisa sat quietly taking in the views and all the time questioning herself as to why she was here and Phil just sang along with the music on the radio.

She remembered they always liked the same music, and country and western was just the best to get them almost dancing in their car seats.

They pulled onto the gravel drive and grey stones shot from under the tyres as the car came to a stop. Lisa took a quick glance around before stepping out.

Walking up the steps of her dream towards the old paint peeling door, Lisa suddenly had reservations. Her heart skipped a beat. She almost felt she was stepping into an unknown future. It was a weird sensation that gripped her; shivers rolled down her back.

Phil opened the door and ushered her in first. She stepped over the threshold and felt very odd, almost like she was entering a film set. She felt she was about to make memories which she hadn't wanted to because they would hurt her later. Had she been the type to be scared of ghosts, she would have run; she almost felt one was there, watching her, laughing at her and Phil who hadn't made their dream happen.

They were soon inside and looking around; to the left of this entrance hall there was a small room, this may have been a study, she was thinking. This hall had ornate pillars holding up a wide circular staircase that drew her eye up to the balcony. The stairs led to five bedrooms and three bathrooms; this she had read in the house details back in Harry's office. She turned to stand close to the bottom step of those stairs, took hold of the banister, lifted her foot and as she did so heard Phil's warning.

"Be careful, the stairs have broken slats."

The wood creaked as she set her foot down and she slipped, hitting her head on the bottom stair.

Suddenly she visualised welcoming people into this massive hall, big enough to hold a small round table with a vase of fresh flowers sitting in its middle. She saw well dressed women coming down the royal blue carpet, gracefully holding up their long evening gowns. They were coming down, to talk with her. A party was being held but she couldn't hear any voices. She left the imaginary crowd and slowly wandered from room to room.

The sitting room had a wow factor with floor to ceiling windows where full length curtains hung with tiebacks. Views of the garden showed a sweeping lawn, mown low with stripes and flower beds enhanced its edges. In its centre a white bird bath stood.

She turned to glance around the room; at the far end a fireplace with a marble surround stood and above it a mantel held a golden clock at its centre. Photos of her grandchildren took their place alongside each other and there was Andy with Beth in her wedding grown. Another picture showed a much younger man who Lisa couldn't recognise.

Regency armchairs sat either side of the fireplace and as she looked up, there hung an oil painting of her sitting in one of those chairs with Phil standing proudly behind, his hand placed on her shoulder. Two dogs, one like Barney and another a golden colour, lay at her feet.

Lisa rubbed at her eyes; she couldn't understand what she was seeing and screamed out.

***

"Lisa, are you okay?" Phil was asking while patting her cheek gently.

"What happened?" she said.

"Your foot tripped on that cracked step at the bottom of the stairs and you hit your head on the wall. You were out cold, only for a few seconds. Are you sure you're all right, or do you want to be checked at the hospital?"

Phil was very concerned; she had gone down with quite a bang and appeared extremely shaken.

She had been in and around this house, she just knew she had. She shook her head, to clear her thoughts.

Had she just seen the future? Walked her dream, right here, right now?

Again she shook her head and Phil asked if she was really sure she didn't need a hospital visit. She smiled back at him from a very pale face and just sat there saying nothing until he took her hand.

"No, I'm fine, really I am," she said and taking the offered hand and using the banister, she rose up from where she had tripped and had that beautiful vision.

Her legs wobbled while she rubbed her head.

"I would like to see the rest of the house, please," she said; she needed to see it.

The kitchen had little left intact but for the red tiled floor and with a little work that could be saved. A refit was required for the rest, though.

She only needed to look in one bathroom and thought, no way would anyone want to get in that bath. It was disgustingly dirty and the enamel was chipped where rust spread in the iron built bath tub.

Two bedrooms sat above that fantastically large empty sitting room and had equally good views of the garden as the downstairs room. The sweeping lawn she had seen in her vision was in actual fact a massive bed of brown dead weeds a foot high, left from the autumn, and the birdbath lay on its side, half buried by that growth.

The other three bedrooms looked out over a curving drive of gravel mixed with more weeds to the front of the house where Phil's car sat.

Lisa was amazed at just how big this house was.

"I wouldn't want to clean this place," she told Phil.

He laughed.

"What?" she asked, looking at him with a puzzled frown.

He wouldn't think to clean this house or any come to that.

"Lisa, if you could afford a house of this size, you would be able to afford people to come in, to clean, cook and do the garden."

"Oh, but I couldn't. I'd have to tidy up before they arrived."

He laughed again, so much so, that all she could do was join him.

"Shut up," and she punched him playfully.

"I'll get you for that," he said as he bent over and pretended to be winded. She ran, with him close on her heels.

Down the stairs Lisa dashed and jumped over that last broken step. Phil was taking the stairs two at a time and was gaining on her. Chasing her out into the garden where they dodged each other around the overgrown bushes. They played at touching each other before running off.

They passed the spring flowers pushing their way through massive clumps of weeds, some new and green, others brown and dried out, left from last year.

Lisa hid behind a massive oak tree trunk. Phil looked around him; he spotted her dog covered patterned scarf blowing out in the breeze.

He appeared to her to be aimlessly wandering up to the tree, swinging his arms loosely at his side in a carefree way as though he couldn't find her. She giggled into her hand and tried to keep quiet.

Then he jumped around the tree and grabbed her from behind. She squealed with delight as his arms surrounded her. Suddenly they were young again; the years had melted away.

He held her close to his chest and with those deep sparkling blue eyes looking down at her, she was putty in his arms.

Time stood still it seemed, even reversed to another time long ago, when she felt warm and safe. With him close again she felt somehow inside her dream.

Their faces slowly touched, lips joined, they kissed long and softly before becoming more intense. He wanted more, but then he always had and now she did too. That's what got them into trouble in the first place all those years ago. Now they were older, wiser, but that made no difference to the yearning inside them both and he gently lowered her to the ground where they embraced some more, kissed and caressed. She felt the button of her blouse pop open and then her skirt move but all Lisa could hear were the birds singing their spring tunes from where they sat in the tops of the trees.

The sun shone down on a happy couple in love and lost in their dream, and the birds were in love too. All Lisa's memories of losing him went flying away like the clouds on the breeze above.

But as she opened her eyes to the sun that dazzled her she suddenly awoke from that dream. She pushed him aside and shouted out. The birds flew from the trees and in their frenzy they chirped and twittered away.

"No! No! I can't do this. Take me back to work," Lisa cried and pushed him off her.

I'm not changing a thing. She remembered her New Year's resolution.

She sprang from the ground like a frightened young girl with her old bullying father watching her as she straightened her clothes.

She ran back to his car and stood panting as she leaned on it. She couldn't think straight. What was she doing? She had to get out of this situation. Their life together had long since finished, gone, lost forever and she panicked that they would never be happy again, not together.

"I'll take you back. I'm sorry," he said as he came dashing up to her.

Phil was like a dog with his tail between his legs. He had blown it, lost her and felt extremely sad as he opened his car door. He moved to hold her hand, he was going to apologise again. "Don't." she said and moved her hand away.

Was it too late? Lisa's eyes filled with tears as she turned her face away from a dejected man and that lovely old house that sat in the background.

A sudden sigh came from deep within her, from nowhere it made its way out from her mouth. He heard but ignored it. Her past had been buried for so long and now she wondered at her dream disintegrating. Could it ever have been theirs? Had she missed her opportunity for happiness? Was she the one who had now thrown their chance away?

***

The drive back to the estate agent was faster than the one to the house. Other than the roar of the car's engine, it was deadly quiet, as both had their own thoughts to deal with. Even the radio had been turned off by Phil.

Lisa jumped out, saying nothing as she had said nothing in the car. Phil shouted goodbye but she didn't respond, didn't even look back.

Running into Ben she yelled at him.

"I have to leave," she told him. "No not early; now, forever."

"Go then; didn't want you here anyway," Ben told her. She gathered her things and with tears now flooding down her face she ran. "Go on; leave us in the middle of the end of year stuff."

She wouldn't be able to come back. Harry was out and this was Ben's chance to dismiss her from her temp job.

Lisa dashed out to the small car park around the back and sped off at an alarming rate, only to take the corner too sharp and dent her car wing on that low post which any other day she passed quite easily.

"Damn!" she cursed but didn't stop to look at any damage done.

She found herself at Margaret's house. She would tell it as it was; no messing with Margaret and her thoughts on any subject. Lisa needed that right now.

"Hello, Lisa; to what do I owe the pleasure?" She stopped in her tracks when she saw Lisa's face. Mascara dribbles reached down to smudged, deep pink lipstick. Her hair was a mess where she had run her fingers though it so many times as she drove.

"Come in, my dear; whatever's happened?" Margaret took Lisa's arm and walked her to the sitting room, noticing the small dried particles of grass and what looked like brown flower heads caught up in her hair.

"Sit. Tell me, would you like a cup of tea?"

"Oh, No more bloody tea! That's all us English ever think of in a crisis. Make tea. Sorry." Lisa looked up at Margaret and cried some more. "What am I going to do?" she mumbled through her tears.

"If you don't tell me, I can't tell you." And with that Margaret leaned forward with a sorrowful face and pulled a collection of grasses from Lisa's hair.

Lisa was now very embarrassed; what was

Margaret thinking? But she still managed to spill all her life out before sitting back, her eyes dry now, clear of emotion and wiped on the many tissues taken from her handbag.

"I see," was Margaret's only reply.

"I see, I see, is that all you can say, I see?" Lisa got up to march around Margaret's sitting room.

Margaret's poor cat, Patch, was hiding under the sofa, unable to cope with all this crying and marching of humans.

"No, not really; I wonder if you do really want my thoughts, my advice or are you just letting off steam."

"Yes, of course I want to hear what you have to say, or I wouldn't be here, would I?"

Lisa shouted, remembering she had left out the part about the roll in the weed patch situation, at the old house. She thought that a little too much information for Margaret to handle. But Margaret wasn't silly. She was old enough to know and had seen much in her lifetime. She had already guessed what had happened, even if she didn't know how far the rough and tumble may have reached.

"Well, sit back down, calm down and let's talk about this, shall we?" Margaret took Lisa's hand and guided her back to the sofa.

She began to tell Lisa how unhappy she had been throughout her long marriage. That she, too, had been pregnant with Mollie when she married and that Mollie didn't know of this and she would be grateful if Lisa said nothing to her about it.

Lisa was taken aback at this information and

nodded in acknowledgement.

She knew that in Margaret's young days, if you became pregnant, you married the boy who got you into *trouble*, as it was called back then. Regardless of who he was, he married the girl unless the parents had the money to send her away to have her baby, which was often taken away from her at birth. Or she was sent to other family members, again miles away. There wasn't all the support given to single mums as there was today.

Those women needed a man's money coming in, to live and eat and perhaps that's why Lisa's aunt did what she did. Lisa's mind was wandering back to her family before she heard Margaret ask how she really felt about Phil.

Before Lisa could answer one question the next came.

"Did you love him? Do you truly love him now? How do you feel knowing the truth as to why he left you and Beth?" Margaret went on. "Have you thought of living the rest of your years alone, into old age, like me?"

The evening wore on. Margaret cooked Lisa dinner and they talked for hours. Lisa could now understand Margaret much better than she ever had before. She had kept baby Mollie and married her late husband.

Lisa realised that early life can sometimes effect how you are in later life. Was this why Margaret was an unhappy lady, sad with her thoughts of a life passed by. Perhaps her history had made her this way and this was why she hadn't shown Mollie much affection. Lisa could now see Margaret loved her daughter but had never hugged or used the words of love to her.

Mollie had told Beth some years before that her mother wasn't like Lisa, there had been no touching or kind words for Mollie when growing up, other than from her father, who had died the year Beth met Mollie.

It had been as though Margaret resented Mollie, blamed her for her life, and that was something Lisa had never done to Beth.

Lisa felt better now and was about to return home when Margaret asked her one final question.

"What are you going to do about Philip?"

"I'm going to tell him I love him."

"Good," was all Margaret would say and she smiled at Lisa as she left.

She almost danced out of Margaret's front door, down the path to find her car. It was now that she took the time to check the dent. She smiled at the damage and thought, that's nothing to the damage I could do to the rest of my life, if I don't tell him.

"I love him!" She shouted it aloud when she was sitting in her car.

Arriving home, Lisa ran up to her door, entered and grabbed hold of Barney and whispered in his floppy ear.

"I'm in love, Barney, and not just with you."

He barked and sat his big old backside down on the envelope which had been posted through her letterbox earlier that day.

There was a red light flashing in her sitting room,

on her home phone. She made a dash to pick it up. A message, from Phil, she immediately thought. But no, it was a message from Harry. He was concerned for her after speaking with Ben and he wasn't going to accept her leaving until he had spoken with her. In fact he had had some strong words with his son over the matter and Ben had been surprised at this.

Lisa was to go in tomorrow and sort things out with both him and Ben.

She was disappointed it hadn't been Phil talking to her and deleted the message. She turned the TV on, this would distract her thoughts. Well that was the idea, only she found herself staring at the home phone, wishing it to ring. Then she rummaged in her bag for her mobile phone. No text or message of any kind. Her i-pad lay on the breakfast bar in the kitchen; nothing there either. Finally she opened her laptop, just in case her i-pad had missed anything. Not one message, from any source and she didn't have his number; her pride had always stopped her asking for it.

But she would get it from Harry tomorrow.

By the time she was preparing for bed she had convinced herself Phil hadn't changed. He had kissed her, loved her and disappeared again.

Just like all men, they only want one thing. She could hear her mother's words haunting her. And she again found tears flowing, not because of not having close loving parents; she had got used to that, but those words from her mother.

She had been young and didn't understand what they meant until later, when womanhood hit and a school friend told her. This had left Lisa feeling embarrassed because she hadn't had any idea. Sex had been a taboo subject with her mother.

She felt so sorry for her mother now for her to think that way.

The home phone suddenly rang making her half jump out of her life. She dashed for it, grabbed it from the coffee table and shouted down it, "hello."

It was only Margaret. Lisa's heart sunk yet again. "Oh, hello."

"Just checking on you; that you arrived home okay," Margaret said. "Have a good night's sleep dear. Bye"

Sleep? How was she going to sleep? Phil hadn't been in touch.

She turned off the lights in the lower half of her house, locked the back door and walked into the hall. She was on her way up to her bed when there, at the bottom of the stairs, she saw a white envelope with dirty paw prints and hair from a black dog stuck all over it.

"Barney, what's this?" And he looked up at her with those big brown eyes, his head tilted to one side.

She opened the envelope and her legs gave way for the second time that day. She fell back onto the stairs after reading the first line.

Darling Lisa.

Barney laid his head on her lap as she read more.

I am so very sorry that I make you unhappy. I don't mean too.

She rubbed at her eyes which were misting up and read more.

I will move out of your life again. Sell the old house and sign the divorce papers. Then you are free to move on. I hope you find happiness, my darling. I will always love you. Phil x

"No!" She screamed out and frightened Barney, who barked at her. She ran her hand down his head and on down his back. He nuzzled his nose under her chin, to lift it.

"Oh, Barney what am I going to do? I love him."

Lisa couldn't sleep that night. In the morning she knew just what she was going to do. See Harry.

Harry almost felt like a father to her these days and he had heard from his wife who lunched with ladies who had a wonderful grapevine between them, gossip, that Lisa hadn't had an easy life.

Lisa had often wanted a father just like Harry; he was old enough to be just that and with his rounded middle and jolly caring smile. Harry wasn't like her father at all, a father she hadn't seen since she married Phil. Phil, she was determined to find Phil.

***

Hurrying to get showered and dressed, she skipped breakfast and pulled herself together. She stood up straight and felt determined by the time she had driven to the estate agency to see Harry. She was now full of positivity, *her life was going to change*, and she was in charge of it.

She knew Harry would be in early and long before Ben, who took his father for granted and lived off his hard work and his money. That made her angry; he should appreciate the good father he had.

"Lisa, I'm so glad you came in and so early," Harry greeted her.

"I have to talk to you about Phil," she told him before he could speak any more. She asked if he knew where he was. But what Harry was telling her made her heart sink lower still. The old house had been put back on the market and already there was an offer on it.

"What? No!" she screamed. "You can't sell it. Hold the sale," she told Harry and then asked him again if he knew where Phil had gone.

"Yes. Southampton," Harry said and smiled at her.

"Have you got his phone number?" Lisa yelled at Harry now, who didn't mind being yelled at, on this occasion. Really he was an old romantic, but never let it be said aloud.

"Well, yes and no," he said.

"What do you mean? You must have." She pleaded with Harry.

"You see his phone fell from his pocket and smashed and he was going to replace it."

Lisa swung around not really knowing where to look.

"What am I going to do?"

"If you leave now, you might just catch him before he leaves the country."

"What? Why is he leaving?" Nothing was making sense to her.

"Ships, drawings," Harry said but she was already dashing out the door with the words ringing in her ears.

She grabbed an overnight bag from under her bed and packed it. She then set off towards Southampton.

Packing the bag was a reaction, in case these items were needed on a night stop over. She would need her wash bag and clean clothes, if not to stay with him, for herself.

As she drove she knew, one way or another, this would be the start of her new life or the very end.

The roads seemed extra busy that day, but perhaps it just seemed that way because she was in a hurry, on a mission to get her man.

It took her hours of driving before she saw the huge ships docked in the Ocean Cruise terminal. The ships rose up higher than the buildings surrounding them. She had never seen such a sight, never realised a ship would stand so tall.

Which ship company would he work for? P and O or Princess or what was that one tucked behind; she couldn't see to read its name. Would he be on a ship or in their offices? Oh dear,

she didn't know that either. Which way should she go? She sat in her car and scanned the area. Where is he? She felt lost as to what to do next.

She saw a car parking space and grabbed it before anyone else could. She placed a ticket inside her car, on the dashboard. Now what? She had to think quickly and decided to go to the man on the gate and ask him where to look.

He wouldn't know people's names he said. He only manned the gates and checked the parking tickets, she should have known that. He raised his cap and rubbed at his bald head. He told her to try the offices on the right and pointed in their direction. If that failed he said perhaps someone else working the docks might know of this man, Mr Phil Kingston.

Yes that's what she would do. Lisa thanked the man.

She ran towards the office blocks and grabbed the handle of the first one she came to. It wouldn't open. She saw the notice stuck on the locked door and stopped to read.

"No!" She shouted, but there was no one there to hear. She stamped her feet like a child when she read that notice.

Closed today for training purposes.

She turned around and searched the area, so many faces, but none she knew. She felt lost and dazed by all the activity of excited people walking passed, some were carrying heavy cases, other cases rattled along on wheels; mothers called to their children, to hurry them along and not to get lost. Baggage handlers were taking those cases. There were so many people; how was she ever going to find Phil?

She asked a security woman standing outside the second office block if she knew Philip Kingston.

"Yes you just missed him. He's gone to a late meeting."

She walked off again, still hoping to find Phil. The tears were building when a voice came from behind her.

"What are you doing here?" Phil asked as he gently touched her shoulder.

Lisa turned around but then said, nonchalantly,

"just looking at ships," and shrugged.

He threw his arms around her and gripped her gently as he lifted her, to swing her feet off the ground.

"Please don't go to the other side of the world and leave me again," she whispered into his neck.

He replaced her feet on the ground.

"Who told you I was leaving the country?"

"Harry."

Phil didn't let her see but he grinned to himself. He knew he was going nowhere: *Harry you old rogue.*

She snuggled up close and he lowered his lips to meet hers; she whispered, "I never stopped loving you."

He had noticed all the people looking at them but Lisa was oblivious to anything around her.

He kissed her gently this time. There was no heated passion in that kiss, just pure soft love, which said it was forever.

"I love you, Lisa," he said.

"I love you, I love you too," she mumbled against his chest.

"How would you like to go on one of those ships?" he asked as he pointed to the one nearest to them.

Lisa could only stand and stare at him in amazement.

"Come on. I know the owners. I'll get a couple of tickets. We will have that honeymoon after all," he said and held her hand.

They ran off hand in hand together like

youngsters would, to the ticket offices on the other side of the buildings, where he knew the right people. He knew there were often empty cabins aboard.

She even had her passport in her overnight bag, left from the girlie weekend she had had with Mollie, on her hen night five years ago. Lisa hadn't travelled far since, she never had the money.

They were on board and looking from the balcony of their suite. Arms draped around each other's waists, they looked out to sea where the gulls swooped by and the golden sun was setting on their past.

It was no good, Lisa had to ask, how he could possibly pay for two first class tickets without saving for years.

Phil kissed her on her forehead, then her nose and lastly a long lingering kiss on those soft lips of hers; he didn't want to spoil the moment and talk about money.

Only he could see in her eyes he would have to tell her.

"My darling, after I left you I went back to college. Got myself a degree and worked hard to save. I have always wanted to return to you and our Beth; I just didn't know how to make it happen. I have my own company and am earning real money now and it's all going to go on you."

She gazed into his eyes.

"I don't need your money; I just need you to stay this time."

"I'm not going anywhere, my love," and he squeezed her close to him. "Money helps though, you know," he said, and laughed while wondering how she thought he had afforded to send Beth money twice a year for so very long.

They were on their way to their future; well a future would be waiting for them on their return but for now they were going to enjoy each other.

The sea was calm and so was Lisa, she felt for the first time in her life that her world would be a safe place.

Phil had already phoned Harry on his replacement phone to put a stop to the sale of their house, their dream and thanked him for not giving Lisa his phone number. He had been a bit sneaky with that, as he had hoped she would go looking for Phil after he told Harry that he had left her that letter.

Their dream house would be waiting for them in three weeks time and they would refit it together as they would refit their married life.

Lisa rang Margaret who just said, "if that's what you want my dear, I'm pleased for you."

She phoned Beth to let them know where she was and asked her to tell Alison and Rosie, she would enjoy her gossiping in the hospital.

She also asked Beth to go and collect Barney and to take good care of him until they got back. Beth could hardly believe her mother's words and ran off to scream at Andy.

"Mum and dad are on their honeymoon!"

J L Appleton
My other books for your consideration
Book one

A true story of a special needs son Love story Fiction
Who would prove he could have
What people like to call a normal life.

Children's story books.

www.jasmine-appleton.co.uk

If you would like to be notified of future publications, please go to
http://eepurl.com/dzM9CL

Printed in Poland
by Amazon Fulfillment
Poland Sp. z o.o., Wrocław